THE GENTLE GIANT

'To hell with them!' Rushton snorted, ignoring the fact that Tiny was now standing up. 'How the son-of-a-bitch are they going to find us?'

The question was, if not answered, at least rendered pointless at that moment!

There was a splintering crackle of breaking timber and Mark Counter literally burst into view through the floorboards!

Even as he was rising, the blond giant's hands dipped to the ivory butts of his Army Colts. Yet, in spite of the speed with which he was moving and the consternation his dramatic appearance was causing most the room's occupants, he realised that his life and that of his new found friend was still dependent upon his two *amigos* being able to carry out their parts in the scheme . . .

Books by J. T. Edson, arranged in chronological order.

Ole Devil Hardin series
YOUNG OLE DEVIL
OLE DEVIL AND THE CAPLOCKS
OLE DEVIL AND THE MULE TRAIN
OLE DEVIL AT SAN JACINTO
GET URREA

The Civil War series
COMANCHE
YOU'RE IN COMMAND NOW, MR FOG
THE BIG GUN
UNDER THE STARS AND BARS
THE FASTEST GUN IN TEXAS
KILL DUSTY FOG!
THE DEVIL GUN
THE COLT AND THE SABRE
THE REBEL SPY
THE BLOODY BORDER
BACK TO THE BLOODY BORDER

The Floating Outfit series
THE YSABEL KID
.44 CALIBRE MAN
A HORSE CALLED MOGOLLAN
GOODNIGHT'S DREAM
FROM HIDE AND HORN
SET TEXAS BACK ON HER FEET
THE HIDE AND TALLOW MEN
THE HOODED RIDERS
QUIET TOWN
TRAIL BOSS
WAGONS TO BACKSIGHT
TROUBLED RANGE
SIDEWINDER
RANGELAND HERCULES
MCGRAW'S INHERITANCE
THE HALF BREED
THE WILDCATS
THE BAD BUNCH
THE FAST GUN
CUCHILO
A TOWN CALLED YELLOWDOG
TRIGGER FAST
THE MAKING OF A LAWMAN
THE TROUBLE BUSTERS
SET A-FOOT
THE LAW OF THE GUN
THE PEACEMAKERS
TO ARMS! TO ARMS! IN DIXIE!
HELL IN THE PALO DURO
GO BACK TO HELL
THE SOUTH WILL RISE AGAIN
THE QUEST FOR BOWIE'S BLADE
BEGUINAGE
BEGUINAGE IS DEAD!
THE RUSHERS
THE FORTUNE HUNTERS
RIO GUNS
GUN WIZARD
THE TEXAN
THE RIO HONDO KID
WACO'S DEBT
THE HARD RIDERS
THE FLOATING OUTFIT
APACHE RAMPAGE
THE RIO HONDO WAR
THE MAN FROM TEXAS
GUNSMOKE THUNDER
THE SMALL TEXAN
THE TOWN TAMERS
RETURN TO BACKSIGHT
TERROR VALLEY
GUNS IN THE NIGHT

Waco series
SAGEBRUSH SLEUTH
ARIZONA RANGER
WACO RIDES IN
THE DRIFTER
DOC LEROY, M.D.
HOUND DOG MAN

Calamity Jane series
COLD DECK, HOT LEAD
THE BULL WHIP BREED
TROUBLE TRAIL
THE COW THIEVES
CALAMITY SPELLS TROUBLE
WHITE STALLION, RED MARE
THE REMITTANCE KID
THE WHIP AND THE WAR LANCE
THE BIG HUNT

Alvin Dustine 'Cap' Fog series
YOU'RE A TEXAS RANGER, ALVIN FOG
'CAP' FOG, TEXAS RANGER, MEET MR. J. G. REEDER

The Rockabye County series
THE SIXTEEN DOLLAR SHOOTER
THE PROFESSIONAL KILLERS
THE ¼ SECOND DRAW
THE DEPUTIES
POINT OF CONTACT
THE OWLHOOT
RUN FOR THE BORDER
BAD HOMBRE

Bunduki series
BUNDUKI
BUNDUKI AND DAWN
SACRIFICE FOR THE QUAGGA GOD
FEARLESS MASTER OF THE JUNGLE*

Miscellaneous titles
SLAUGHTER'S WAY
TWO MILES TO THE BORDER
SLIP GUN
J.T.'S HUNDREDTH
J.T.'S LADIES*
BLONDE GENIUS (*written in collaboration with Peter Clawson*)

* *Awaiting publication by Corgi Books.*

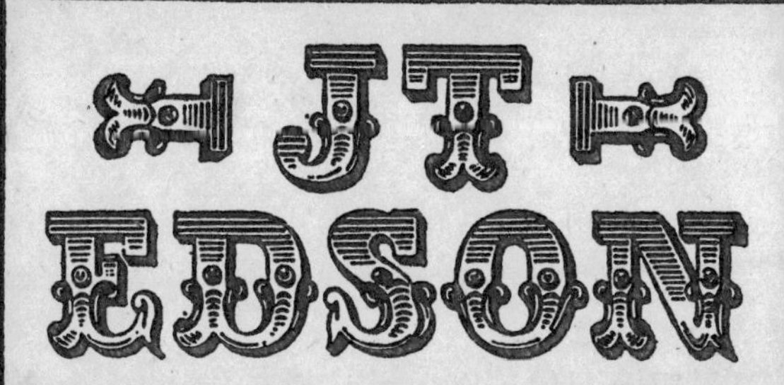

THE GENTLE GIANT

CORGI BOOKS
A DIVISION OF TRANSWORLD PUBLISHERS LTD

THE GENTLE GIANT

A CORGI BOOK 0 552 11224 0

First publication in Great Britain

PRINTING HISTORY
Corgi edition published 1979

This book is set in 10/10½pt Baskerville

Corgi Books are published by Transworld Publishers Ltd.,
Century House, 61–63 Uxbridge Road,
Ealing, London W5 5SA.
Made and printed in Great Britain by
Hunt Barnard Printing Ltd., Aylesbury, Bucks.

For our Ann and Cousin Tom Stansbury,
not forgetting their undersized vulture
and 'orrible dog.

AUTHOR'S NOTE

While complete in itself, this volume continues from the events recorded in THE MAKING OF A LAWMAN and THE TROUBLE BUSTERS. Once again, to save my old hands from repetition and for the benefit of new readers, we are giving the history and special qualifications of Dusty Fog, Mark Counter, the Ysabel Kid and Waco in the form of appendices.

We also realise that, in our present 'permissive society' we could employ the actual profanities used by various people who appear in this book, but we do not concede that a spurious desire to create 'realism' is a valid reason for doing so. Lastly, with the exception of calibres appropriate to certain weapons – i.e. Luger 9 mm. automatic pistol – we have no intention of following the current 'trendy' pandering to the exponents of the metric system and will continue to employ miles, yards, feet, inches, pounds and ounces when referring to distances and weights.

J. T. EDSON

CHAPTER ONE

YOU 'N' ME COULD MAYBE HOIST HER UP

'God-damn it to hell and back again by the long trail!' Town Marshal Kail Beauregard ejaculated in what could only be described as a speeded up, yet *sotto voce* Southern drawl, as he pushed his way through the crowd on the sidewalk in front of Henry's Saloon with less than the courtesy he would usually have displayed. '*This's* all I need today of *all* god-blasted days.'

The last three words might have struck some people as being a highly unacceptable way for a law enforcement officer to be referring to the Fourth of July, the day upon which loyal citizens of the United States of America celebrated the gaining of independence from British domination back in 1776. His words could even have implied a lack of patriotism. There was, however, what any fair minded person who knew the whole circumstances would regard as adequate justification for the speaker's comment. He might, in fact, have been excused if he had employed even stronger terms to describe his predicament; particularly as the words were intended for no ears other than his own.

Six foot tall, well made and in his late thirties, Beauregard was brown haired. His face, with a neatly trimmed moustache, was tanned by long exposure to the elements and was ruggedly handsome, only rarely allowing its emotions to show. Although his bearing and carriage suggested he was a horseman possessing military training – which was correct as he had been a captain in the Army of the Confederate States during the War of Secession – he wore a smart grey three-piece suit, a white shirt and sober dark blue necktie of a well-to-do town dweller and his brown boots were more suitable for walking than riding. His low crowned, wide brimmed black J. B. Stetson hat was indicative of origins to the south of Kansas, however, being shaped after the fashion most favoured by the Texans who brought their herds of half wild longhorn cattle to the railroad's shipping pens and, by doing so, provided the town of Mulrooney with one of its major sources of income. There was an aura of competence and self-control about him, despite the latter being somewhat disturbed at that moment. It implied he was a man with whom it would be unwise to trifle and the well worn ivory handled Colt 1860 Army revolver he carried reposed in the fast draw holster of a capably designed and manufactured gunbelt.

Up until coming upon the sight which provoked the irate comment, the marshal had been in the best of spirits and temper. The weather was fine, being neither too hot nor too windy. It was, in fact, ideal for the official ceremony which was soon to be commenced. Nor had he found anything to cause concern while making a tour of the main street, to satisfy himself that all was well prior to joining the other civic dignitaries. Despite various saloons and other places dispensing liquor having been open for at least two hours, there was everywhere an atmosphere of amiability and none of the drunken rowdiness or hostility which would need to be quelled by the municipal peace officers. Nor, believing it would be out of the way before the festivities started, had he been particularly worried at first by seeing a heavily loaded wagon approaching along the street. Then somebody in the crowd had thrown a couple of firecrackers and the detonations spooked the team. Although the driver had managed to bring the horses under control, it was not before they had swerved, causing the right side rear wheel to come off its axle, thus halting the vehicle at an angle that practically blocked the thoroughfare. What was more, in spite of there being a large number of onlookers present, none of them was doing anything more constructive than standing and staring when Beauregard arrived on the scene.

'Whee-dogie, *amigo*,' remarked a member of the crowd who, although they were on terms of close acquaintance, the marshal had pushed by without noticing while delivering his wrathful comment. Being cognisant with the pressures which were causing the newly appointed head of Mulrooney's municipal law enforcement agency to display such uncharacteristic emotions in public, he walked forward as he continued speaking. 'Looks like you-all could maybe use some help.'

'Well now!' the peace officer replied, swinging his gaze to the speaker and, helped by the lazy-sounding, yet friendly, deep Texan tones beginning to regain his self control. 'I reckon I just *might* at that. The Independence Day Grand Parade's going to start off any minute now. It'll be coming around that bend and through here to where the Governor of the Sovereign State of Kansas, Her Ladyship Mayor Freddie Woods, the City Fathers and all those railroad high mucky-mucks who've been invited over to see what a fine town we've got, so they'll run their spur-line from here up to Stokeley, Montana, are all sat patient in the sun just waiting for it to happen. Yes sir, Mr Counter, sir, I reckon's how you're justified in saying I could use some help.'

'That being so, we'd best see what we can come up with,' suggested the man to whom the tirade had been directed, showing no sign of animosity. 'Just say what you want doing and we'll give her a whirl.'

A good three inches taller than the marshal, Mark Counter would have stood out in any crowd. In his early twenties, he had recently cut curly golden blond hair[1] and he had a tanned, almost classically handsome face. There was a tremendous spread to his shoulders that tapered to a slender waist set upon long and powerful legs, implying a strength far in excess of the average. From his white, Texas-style Stetson, encircled by a black leather band decorated with silver conchas and sporting a fancy *barbiquejo* chinstrap, through his tight rolled green silk bandana, open necked tan shirt and Levi's pants – the cuffs of their legs turned back to a depth of about three inches – to his fancy stitched, high heeled, sharp toed black boots with spurs on their heels, his garments were all made of the finest materials. With the exception of the pants and the hat, they had clearly been

[1] The author suspects that the trend in movies made since the mid-sixties to portray all cowhands as long haired and filthy has risen less from the producers' desire for 'realism' than because that was the only kind of player available. In our extensive reference library, we cannot find a dozen photographs of cowboys – as opposed to Army scouts, mountain men, or prospectors who have long hair and bushy beards. In fact, our reading on the subject has led us to assume the term 'long hair' was one of derision and opprobrium in the cattle country then as it is today. J.T.E.

tailored to fit his Herculean frame. Around his waist was an exceptionally fine brown *buscadero* gunbelt carrying two ivory handled Army Colts in its contoured, tied-down holsters which were positioned just right to permit a *very* rapid withdrawal if the need arose.

Large the blond giant might be, remarkably strong he undoubtedly was, but there was nothing slow or cumbersome about him. In fact, he gave the impression of being a man who could move with considerable speed when such was called for. He had frequently proved to be capable of doing just that.[2]

'Hey, Mark!' called one of the Texas cowhands in the crowd, before Beauregard could speak, filled with pride at being able to demonstrate he was acquainted with such a prominent son of the Lone Star State. 'Why don't you-all just take hold of that old wagon 'n' hoist it up like you did for Calamity Jane that time?'

There was a rumble of excited and anticipatory agreement from among the other onlookers, many of whom had heard of the incident to which the speaker was referring.[3] Those of the remainder who had come to know the handsome blond giant during the recently ended period when he was serving as first deputy in the town marshal's office,[4] even if they had been disinclined to believe he really had performed the feat in question, were aware of his physical capabilities and hoped to see these demonstrated. The few who did not recognise him, or had drawn an erroneous conclusion with regards to his identity, also waited with interest to see how he would respond to his fellow Texan's suggestion.

Listening to the cowhand's comment and noticing how it had been received, Mark was far from pleased. While he wished to help and could appreciate fully the dilemma that the mishap was creating for the peace officer, he had no desire to have so much thrust upon him and he wanted the

[2] New readers can find details of Mark Counter's background and special qualifications in *APPENDIX TWO*. J.T.E.

[3] Told in: *Part One, 'The Bounty On Belle Starr's Scalp'*, *TROUBLED RANGE* and *CALAMITY, MARK AND BELLE*. J.T.E.

[4] Details of Mark Counter's period as first deputy in the Mulrooney Town Marshal's Office are given in: *THE MAKING OF A LAWMAN* and *THE TROUBLE BUSTERS*. J.T.E.

means by which the wagon was to be removed to be decided by Beauregard.

Any Southerner appointed as marshal of a trail-end, railroad town in Kansas was likely to have his conduct subjected to considerably more critical scrutiny than might be directed at a man whose origins were north of the Mason-Dixon line.[5] In Beauregard's case, he would have the further disadvantage of having his actions compared with the manner in which his predecessor in office had performed similar duties, and the standards set by Dusty Fog had been high. So, despite sympathising with a man who had been a good friend for many years, and while willing to do everything within his power to assist, the blond giant had no wish for people to think Beauregard needed to call upon the previous incumbents of the marshal's office as soon as he was faced with his first emergency.

However, a glance at the peace officer's face told Mark he did not need to worry on that account. Under the circumstances, Beauregard was only too pleased to accept aid from any source. Nor could any fair-minded person blame him for being willing to take it when offered.

The problem facing the blond giant was how he might best assist the marshal. Until the wheel was replaced, the wagon could not be moved. Before this could be done, the axle must be raised to a level at which the hub could be slid on. It would take time to procure a suitable lever for the task and time was one thing they were lacking. Already the band was striking up ready to lead the Grand Parade for which the town's population and visiting dignitaries were waiting. Everybody would be bitterly disappointed and the more influential citizens who had organised the event, not all of whom had been in favour of Beauregard's appointment, would feel humiliated should the accident be allowed to delay it. There would be those who tried to lay the blame upon him and, by doing so, weaken his authority.

In spite of having performed the feat mentioned by the

[5] 'Mason-Dixon' line: sometimes erroneously called the 'Mason-Dixie' line. The boundary between Pennsylvania and Maryland, as surveyed in 1763–67 by the Englishmen Charles Mason and Jeremiah Dixon, which came to be regarded as the dividing line separating the Southern 'Slave' and the Northern 'Free' States of America. J.T.E.

cowhand, Mark knew it had been under different and more favourable conditions. No matter how Calamity Jane might tell the story – and he knew it would be in a manner most creditable to him, if almost certainly exaggerated – she had not been driving her six-horse Conestoga wagon, similar to the one before him, on the day in question. Not only was the vehicle she had been handling then considerably smaller, the load it was carrying was far lighter. So any attempt at duplicating the exploit was practically doomed to failure. Furthermore, because of the crowd's curiosity, other methods which could prove more successful were sure to be held in abeyance while he was trying to lift the wagon no matter how much the marshal wanted them to be carried out.

'Ain't usually the one to come billing in unasked to other folk's doings, gents,' commented a voice as deep as the blond giant's, yet with a mild and almost apologetic timbre to its pronounced Southern drawl, before any further suggestions could be made. 'Only I reckon's how you 'n' me could maybe hoist her up enough for the wheel to be put back on, was we to give it a whirl.'

Ambling with leisurely seeming haste from the crowd, looking like a buffalo bull passing through a herd of pronghorns,[6] the speaker approached Mark and Beauregard. To say he was big would be an understatement.

Matching the blond giant in height, the newcomer was only fractionally more slender across the shoulders and, as he did not trim down so noticeably at the waist, weighed in excess of the other's two hundred and twenty pounds. Unless the way in which the material of his somewhat tight fitting buckskin shirt and trousers pulsated as he moved was lying, the extra weight was caused by hard muscles rather than fat. He had on a brimless, flat-topped cap made from the silver tipped brown skin of a grizzly bear, from beneath which

[6] Despite sometimes being referred to as an 'antelope' and occupying a similar ecological niche in North America to those species qualifying for the title in Africa and Asia, the pronghorn, *Antilocapra Americana*, to a certain extent forms an intermediate group between the deer and the hollow-horned ruminants. The forked horns occur only in the males and the horny sheath is shed every year, leaving the unbranched core naked. Hairy skin grows over the core and forms a new, thin, horny sheath. For added information regarding the pronghorn, see: *THE BIG HUNT*. J.T.E.

showed close cropped black hair. A neatly trimmed beard and moustache set off a set of amiable features tanned to the consistency of old leather by a life which was obviously spent predominently out of doors. Although well worn, his clothes and knee length Pawnee moccasins were clean and tidy. In his massive right hand, a Sharps Old Reliable buffalo gun seemed no larger than a Winchester carbine and the enormous bowie knife sheathed at the left side of his Indian-made waist belt appeared almost diminutive when compared with his bulk.[7]

All in all, if anybody could help Mark lift the wagon, the speaker looked as if he was the one to do it. Yet, despite being in his late twenties, he also conveyed the impression of being a little boy attending his first grown-up party and wanting only to do the right things to please the other guests.

'It's worth a try, Kail,' Mark declared, studying the newcomer's massive frame. 'If we can pull it off, there'll be no call to stop the parade until the wagon's moved. Anyways, we've got nothing to lose by giving it a whirl.'

'Like you say, *amigo*,' Beauregard replied, also subjecting the newcomer to scrutiny and equally impressed by his obviously muscle-packed bulk. 'We've got nothing to lose. But, hoping I don't give offence to either of you-all, I'll send somebody to find a pole we can use as a lever just in case you can't hoist the god-damned thing up.'

'I was hoping you'd decide on something like that,' Mark drawled cheerfully, starting to unbutton his shirt. 'Get your man sent, then make sure the brake's on and have Mr Walton hold his team steady. Soon's all that's done, friend, what say you and me give it a whirl?'

'I'm ready when you are,' declared the gigantic newcomer.

While the marshal was carrying out the suggestions and giving instructions to various members of the crowd whose help would be required if the lifting was successful, Mark peeled off his shirt. Hanging it on the hitching rail alongside where the bearded man was leaning the Sharps rifle, he led the way to the rear of the wagon.

Waiting until the driver – who was also the owner of the

[7] For the dimensions which a 'bowie' knife could attain and other information pertaining to this type of weapon, see, *Footnote Six, APPENDIX THREE.* J.T.E.

vehicle and a prominent local businessman – had checked the brake, and gone to hold the heads of the two lead horses, Mark and the newcomer took up their positions. Placing their backs against the tailgate, it became apparent to the majority of the onlookers that they both knew how best to set about their task. Each hooked his hands beneath the bed of the wagon, but clearly had no intention of relying solely upon his deltoid, bicep and forearm muscles, massive as these were. Instead, they spread their feet slightly apart and bent their knees so that they could bring into play all the power of their backs, buttocks, thighs and calves and thus supplement the force to be applied via their arms.

On receiving a word of command from Beauregard, the blond giant and his assistant began to lift. However, except for the pressure being exerted from within causing the ample sleeves of the newcomer's buckskin to expand under the strain until the material appeared almost paper thin, nothing appeared to be happening.

* * * * *

Not every member of the crowd along the sidewalk in front of Henry's Saloon was finding the attempt to move the loaded wagon by muscle power alone to be an event of absorbing interest. At least one person present considered that far more worthy of attention was the large and bulky pack which the bearded man had set down in the alley alongside the building prior to going forward and offering his assistance.

Human nature being what it is, every town that attracted an ever changing assortment of people, many of whom carried quantities of money in their possession, invariably also attracted people who arrived with the intention of relieving the others of at least a proportion of their wealth by dishonest means. Nor, even with the kind of efficient law enforcement for which it had become famous during its short existence, had it been possible to exclude such undesirable visitors from Mulrooney.

Reg Wall was one such undesirable visitor. Of medium height, lean, with long and oily brownish hair, he had a rat-like set of features which did him an injustice if they were not indicative of a sly and vicious nature. He sported the attire of a buffalo hunter. However, despite the blood-stiffened black jacket, a discoloured U.S. Cavalry *kepi*, a grubby dark blue shirt and matching, yellow-striped riding breeches – which had originated from the same source as the hat, although he had never served in the Army – ending in the knee-high leggings of filthy Osage moccasins, he was not a member of that ignoble fraternity. Born and raised on the Lower East Side of New York, being a petty thief by choice, he was employing the garments as a means of mingling inconspicuously among the populations of the towns west of the Mississippi River. Since coming west and acquiring the clothes, he had on occasion put the Colt 1851 Navy revolver holstered on the right side of his gunbelt and the curved skinning knife sheathed at its left to aggressive purposes; but never in what could be termed fair combat, or against a person who was ready to meet his attack.

Being a pickpocket of some ability, crowds always exercised an attraction to Wall and he was drawn to them like iron filings to a magnet. When passing through one his hands, being devoid of any roughening and stiffening such as would have accrued if he had ever done any hard work, would delve into pockets or vanity bags and extract the contents without the owners realising that their property had been removed until it was too late.

Never an early riser, Wall had not reached Trail Street until shortly before the fireworks had caused the mishap to the wagon. A quick glance around had caused him to congratulate himself upon having found such a potentially lucrative state of affairs. The crowd was not so dense as to make passing through it difficult, but there were sufficient people present to make them less suspicious when being bumped into or jostled by him.

Commencing his activities by removing a silk handkerchief and a thick pocketbook expensively bound in red morocco leather from a corpulent and well dressed man, Wall did not trouble to examine the latter's contents before thrusting it and the handkerchief into the capacious pocket of his jacket. However, as he was on the point of turning his attention to his victim's attractive female companion, he discovered that Mark Counter and Marshal Kail Beauregard were close by.

The new marshal was still an unknown quantity as far as Wall was concerned, but he was aware that while in office the blond giant had proved to be a most competent and efficient peace officer. So he decided against continuing his depredations in their immediate vicinity. Moving along the sidewalk with the intention of seeking his prey in a safer locality, he had seen the pack set down and left unattended by its owner. As nobody appeared to be keeping a watch on it, he had amended his plans.

Sidling up to the pack as if it was the last thing in the world to be of any interest to him, Wall gave it a surreptitious and tentative nudge with his foot. It remained so immovable against the shove that it might have been fastened to the ground. Drawing conclusions from what he had felt, he found himself on the horns of a dilemma. Such was its size and bulk that, despite the apparent ease with which its owner had handled it, he doubted whether he could carry it away. Certainly he could not hope to do so with the alacrity that the theft would require. Nor, studying the expertly secured diamond-hitch lashings, did he consider it would be possible for him to unfasten the knots and remove some of the contents as quickly as the situation demanded.

An easy solution to the problem sprang to the pickpocket's mind. For all its secure fastenings, the pack's cover was nothing more substantial than a waterproof tarpaulin. While stout enough to stand up to rough handling of a conventional kind, he had the means with which to make a way through so he could reach in and remove at least a proportion of whatever it held. A quick glance told him that everybody appeared to be watching the attempt to lift the wagon. So he drew his knife and, standing with his back to the crowd, began to put his scheme into operation.

CHAPTER TWO

THEY'LL *NEVER* DO IT!

'Excuse me, young man, but would you be from that part of Texas which is adjacent to the Mexican border?'

Not everybody in Mulrooney was foregathered along Trail Street to watch the Grand Parade, as the words being spoken near the railroad depot indicated.

The request for information was being made by a tall, good looking, grey haired man of distinguished demeanour who was clad to the height of Eastern big city fashion, including a shining black walking cane with a silver knob for a handle. His companion, to whom he had been speaking in a somewhat heated manner, was of a far less prepossessing appearance and it seemed unlikely that they were on terms of close acquaintance.

Roughly the same age, somewhere between the mid-forties and fifties, the second man's attire was that of a Mexican *vaquero* who had fallen upon hard times. Far from improved by a long scar down the left cheek, his swarthy features and drooping black moustache were indicative of a Hispanic birthright. Although his *charro* clothes had been costly when new, they showed signs of long use and the leather band around his *sombrero* had lost some of the silver conchas which once decorated it. Significantly, the only items which showed signs of having care and attention were the fighting knife and a Freeman Army revolver hanging from his gunbelt.

There was sufficient reason for the speaker to have drawn the conclusions which had prompted his query. However, unless he had made a fortunate guess, it implied he possessed a knowledge pertaining to the dress and habits of people west of the Mississippi River that was not in accord with his clothing and New England accent, each equally suggestive of Eastern origins.

Everything about the person to whom the question was addressed would have informed anybody who knew the West that he was either a Texas cowhand, or had very successfully contrived to make himself look like one. Not yet out of his teens unless appearances were deceptive, just over six foot in height, with a powerful physique filling out to manhood, he was a tanned, handsome, blue-eyed blond. Although his garments were not new, they were neat and had recently been cleaned. From the black stetson to the typical footwear, they were the epitome of what a worker in the cattle business chose to wear if he wanted to be in keeping with his contemporaries and prove himself to be a son of the Lone Star State. Around his waist was a plain, but – to eyes capable of reading the signs – *very* functional brown *buscadero* gunbelt with a brace of staghorn handled Army Colts in holsters, the latter having their bases fastened to his thighs by pigging thongs.

'Well no, sir,' the cowhand replied, with a drawling timbre to his voice which demonstrated beyond any doubt he was from Texas. 'I can't truthful-like come right out and tell you-all I am.'

'Drat it, how unfortunate!' the distinguished-looking Easterner exclaimed, tapping the ferrule of his cane almost petulantly on the planks of the sidewalk. 'I was hoping you could speak some Spanish.'

'I can *habla* a might of Mex', happen it's needed,' the blond youngster drawled, sounding more ashamed than proud of the accomplishment, hooking his thumbs through the armholes of his brown and white calfskin vest. 'Which I've been told comes close to Spanish.'

'It does, my young friend, it most assuredly does,' the grey-haired man declared, exuding relief, while the Mexican stood to one side watching and listening with an apparent lack of comprehension. 'The two languages are, to all intents and purposes, practically identical.'

'Do tell?' the Texan said and, having darted what seemed to be a contemptuous glance at the silent *vaquero*, went on, 'Would you-all be wanting me to do some talking Mex' to the greaser?'

'If you would be so kind, sir,' the Easterner requested. 'He's been following me ever since we left the west-bound train and trying to tell me something. Possibly it is nothing of any great importance, but I feel one should always show civility to visitors in our great and fair country, don't you?'

'Us Texans surely showed some to that son-of-a-bitch Santa Anna and his stinking greaser pack afore we run 'em clean back across the Rio Grande back in 'Thirty-six,' the blond announced, although he was far too young to have been involved in the incident to which he referred,[1] his demeanour suggesting he did not agree with the older man's sentiments as far as Mexican visitors were concerned. 'What do you-all want saying?'

'Would you ask him what he wants, please?' the Easterner inquired.

'Why sure, happen that's what *you* want,' the Texan replied. Having done as requested and listened to the Mexican's explanation, he interpreted it. 'Seems's how he's got something he wants to sell.'

'What is it?' the Easterner asked.

'This,' the Texan answered, displaying a gold pendant which he had been given on posing the question in the *vaquero*'s native tongue.

'Good heavens!' the Easterner ejaculated, taking and examining the object. 'This is *very* good. Ask him where he got it from, please.'

'Allows it belonged to his mother,' the Texan drawled, giving a disbelieving sniff, having once again addressed the Mexican. 'Was I asked, I'd say the son-of-a-bitch's wide-looped it from somebody.'

'Perhaps he's telling the truth, though,' the Easterner suggested, sounding as if he was trying to convince himself or justify his next words. 'Anyway, will you find out how much he wants for it, please?'

'Fifty dollars,' the Texan translated, on acquiring the information. 'I'd say it's likely worth a whole heap more.'

'It is,' the Easterner admitted. 'But see if he'll take twenty-five.' Handing over the sum he had offered when it had finally been agreed upon with only a brief attempt on the part of the Mexican to obtain more, he went on, 'Ask him if

[1] Information regarding the struggles of the colonists in Texas to free themselves from Mexican domination is given in the *Ole Devil Hardin* series. J.T.E.

he has anything else he wants to sell, please.'

'He's got whatever's in here,' the Texan said, at the conclusion of a short conversation with the *vaquero*, having been given a small buckskin pouch. Pouring the contents into the the older man's cupped hands, he continued, 'Whee-dogie! Are them things for real *diamonds*?'

'That they are,' the Easterner confirmed. 'As fine as I've ever seen and I'm a dealer in jewellery. You may have heard of me, Julian Rickmansworth? My shop is famous throughout the whole of Massachusetts.'

'Can't say's I have,' the Texan confessed, but did not offer to introduce himself. 'Anyways, he wants to know how much you'll pay for them. Happen he doesn't know no more about them than he did about that fancy gold doohickey he let you have so cheap, could be you'll get them the same way.'

'It's a possibility,' Rickmansworth conceded soberly 'Although I'm not in the habit of taking advantage of the ignorance of others, young man.'

'Hell, he's nothing but a greaser and likely wide-looped them from somebody else in the first place,' the blond answered. 'Which being, you-all've every right to get 'em off him as cheap's you can.' A crafty grin came to his face as he went on. 'Say though, I've got the rest of my pay from the drive we brought in coming to me and would surely take kind to being able to tote along home something's fancy as some of them diamonds. So I reckon I'll sit in on the game.'

'*You?*' the Easterner asked, frowning.

'Lil ole me,' the Texan agreed.

'Well I – !' Rickmansworth began.

'Put it this way, *mister*,' the youngster interrupted grimly. 'Happen I'm *not* cut in on the pot, I'll get so riled 'n' ornery I'll just natural have to tell the greaser about the joker in it.'

'I don't follow you!' the Easterner blustered, although he knew what was meant by the terms applicable to a game of poker.

'I'll tell him how you-all've cut the ground from under his feet on the price you paid for that gold doohickey, for starters,' the youngster elaborated. 'And's how, happen he's so minded, I can help him find somebody's'll be ready to pay him a *fair* price for the diamonds.'

'Very well,' Rickmansworth assented, giving a shrug of

resignation. 'But I warn you that it will cost a considerable sum to purchase this many stones.'

'I could take him to some cattle buyers's could likely afford 'em, or my boss comes to that,' the Texan countered. 'Only I'm not wanting to cut you out, seeing's how you-all found him first. That wouldn't be right dealing. Let's see what we can get him to take for 'em, then I'll figure out how much of the pot you-all can cut me in for.'

'It's a pity we couldn't have got them for less, although they're worth at least triple what he's accepted,' the Easterner remarked jovially, at the conclusion of a brief discussion in Spanish. 'I assure you, as a jeweller of long standing, fifty dollars each is a bargain neither of us is likely to see repeated in a hurry. How many do you want to take?'

'I'll have four, only you'll have to wait a couple of minutes or so.'

'Why do I have to wait?'

'I don't have two hundred dollars on me,' the Texan replied, glancing to where the Mexican – having been paid by the Easterner – was slouching around the corner of the building in front of which they were standing. 'But my boss's dickering with his buyer at the other side of the tracks and I'll get some of what he's holding for me.'

'Very well,' Rickmansworth replied reluctantly. 'But I wouldn't tell him why you want the money, if I was you. As you pointed out, these diamonds might have been stolen and we could find ourselves in serious difficulties in that case should the police learn of our transaction.'

'You're right's the Injun side of a hoss,' the Texan conceded. 'Only don't figure on quitting the *remuda* while I'm gone. I know this town better'n you-all and I'll come looking for you, with some of my *amigos* along to help me pick up your toes.'[2]

[2] 'Pick up your toes': a colloquialism meaning to inflict punishment. It was derived from the cowhands' roping term meaning to make a catch by throwing the lariat's loop so as to trap an animal's forefeet while it was in motion. Generally, the method was employed to punish a horse which persisted in breaking out of the wrangler's rope corral when part of a *remuda*. While dangerous to carry out, the throw was used on the basis of 'kill or cure'. The other members of the *remuda* could pick up the habit if the offender was allowed to go unchecked. A description of how the throw was made and its effect is given in: *TRAIL BOSS*. J.T.E.

'I'll be right here when you return,' Rickmansworth promised.

'Smart young bastard, wasn't he?' the Mexican remarked, speaking fluent English, as he came from around the corner after the Texan had disappeared into the railroad depot.

'Aren't they *all*?' the Easterner replied, showing no surprise at hearing the other employing his native tongue. 'I told you he was worth taking, "Spanish". He's giving us two hundred dollars and didn't even want to have the diamonds valued, or as much as ask to see some proof that I'm who and what I said I am.'

'Do you reckon he'll come looking for us when he finds out he's bought four hunks of glass?' the Mexican inquired.

'If he does, it'll be alone,' the Easterner guessed. 'He'll be too humiliated to go to the police, or tell his friends he's been rooked. And, if he finds us, I think between my cane and your gun, we can stop him complaining.'

* * * * *

'They'll *never* do it!' a blue-clad young soldier declared, standing among the crowd and watching the two men attempting to lift the heavily loaded wagon.

'You-all wouldn't want to be putting a bet on it, now would you, blue-belly?' challenged the Texas cowhand who had made the suggestion regarding how the mishap could be handled. 'Mark Counter there's just about the strongest man in the whole god-damned world and, from the looks of it, that big jasper helping him could run him a pretty close second.'

'Well they still can't do it!' the soldier insisted, but he sounded just a trifle less certain.

'I've got twenty lil ole iron men here's says they *can* and *will*,' the cowhand asserted, eagerly dipping into his Levi's pocket with his right hand, but never taking his gaze from the object of his attention. 'You-all want to cover it?'

Knowing he did not have a sufficient sum of money to accept the bet, the soldier glanced around in the hope that he might see a friend from whom he could request a loan. Failing to do so, he turned his gaze to the front. Nothing had changed, except that the faces of the two big men were showing the tremendous strain they were under and were being bathed with freely-flowing perspiration to attest to their exertions. Deciding that the bet was as good as won, he recommenced his attempt to locate somebody from whom he might obtain the required twenty dollars. Then he heard sharp intakes of breath bursting simultaneously from the people about him. Snapping his gaze back to the centre of attraction, he could scarcely believe the evidence of his eyes.

At first, there was only a slight quiver of motion from the wagon!

Then, slowly but surely and to the accompaniment of concerted gasps and exclamations of amazement from the onlookers, the end of the vehicle began to rise!

Inch after inch, the tilt of the wagon's bed decreased until it once more became level!

However, the two big men's Herculean task was not yet over!

The trouble had been caused by the unexpected swerve causing the wheel-nut to come off, which in turn allowed the hub to slip from the rear axle. Once liberated, the wheel had trundled away until falling in the street. Sent by Marshal Kail Beauregard, two men had already retrieved and returned with it. Holding it vertically, they were holding it ready to slide it into position on the axle. A third man had found and would replace the nut when this had been done.

'Just a mite higher, fellers!' Beauregard requested, although he had hardly believed Mark and the burly, bearded newcomer could even have achieved as much as had already been done.

Holding the heads of the two lead horses as he had been instructed, Ezra Walton was just as amazed by the discovery that the pair had managed to lift the wagon. He was less pleased by the prospect of the wheel being replaced than might have been expected by anybody who was unaware of the circumstances.

Being one of the faction in Mulrooney who had opposed the appointment of Beauregard, Walton had deliberately engineered the mishap. He had hoped it would cause embarrassment for and a loss of faith in the new marshal. At first, like the soldier, he had not believed anything positive would come of the blond and black bearded giants' efforts other than creating a further delay which could be added to the complaints made against the peace officer's handling of the affair.

Discovering he was in error with the assumption brought a scowl of annoyance to Walton's surly face. Then he saw a way out of the dilemma. Already made restless by the firecrackers thrown by an accomplice and not the best trained he owned, the team were only kept motionless by his control. If he should relax his hold on the lead pair's heads, they would all move forward. Not much, perhaps, but sufficient, even with the brake on, for his purpose of causing the men at the rear to lose their hold. He felt sure they would not be able to repeat their remarkable feat if they should be compelled to drop the enormous burden. In fact, the sudden and unexpected cessation of their efforts was likely to produce injuries which would render the recipients incapable of trying a second time.

The latter point did not deter Walton from his decision to put the scheme into effect!

Something else did, however!

'If that wagon moves, Mr Walton, *you* won't,' warned a voice charged with menace, from the driver's rear. 'At least, not until you get carried off by the doctor.'

Identifying the owner of the grimly spoken tones even before he looked over his shoulder, Walton refrained from carrying out his intentions. While he had not the slightest objection to causing suffering to others, he drew the line at having anything of that nature inflicted upon himself and he had no doubt it would be if he should allow the horses to move.

While the man standing a short distance away might be wearing the attire of a successful professional gambler, nothing about his tone or demeanour suggested he might be merely bluffing. Nor, unless Walton had been misinformed with regards to its secondary purpose, was the shiny black stick he held before him in both hands a simple aid to walking. In the hands of a person who had served as another of Dusty Fog's deputy marshals and was therefore a good friend of Mark Counter, it could be converted into a deadly weapon which its owner would not hesitate to use if he was offered suitable provocation.[3]

Standing as tense as a cougar waiting to pounce on a passing whitetail deer, Frank Derringer was in deadly earnest. Tall, slimly built yet anything except puny, brownish haired and good looking, his chosen profession prevented him from acquiring the tan of an outdoors' man, a fact which did nothing to detract from his ability in times of danger. A low crowned, wide brimmed, white 'planter's' hat tilted on the back of his head. His well-cut grey cutaway coat, frilly bosomed white silk shirt, fancy shot-silk vest, yellowish-brown nankeen trousers and shining black town boots attested to his prosperity. Slanting downwards from his left hip, an equally well polished black gunbelt carrying an ivory hilted Army Colt in its tied-down, contoured holster indicated his elegant appearance was not detrimental to the possession of skill in matters of self-preservation or enforcing his will upon others when the need arose.

A shrewd judge of character, as befitted one who had attained success in his selected line of endeavour, Derringer had had the added advantage of knowing something of Walton's sentiments and stated intentions with regard to Beauregard's appointment as town marshal. So he had been suspicious when he saw the loss of the wagon's wheel at such an unpropitious moment. Instead of accompanying Mark and the marshal, or mentioning his suspicion to a third companion whose attention appeared to be directed elsewhere, he had watched the businessman with considerable care. What he had deduced from the sullen face had warned him that his concern could be justified. Although thankful that he had taken up a position from which his warning would carry the greatest impact, it was not until he saw Walton's exasperated and alarmed glare that he realised just how well timed his words had been. However, in spite of the other's obvious anger, he was confident he had prevented something taking place that could not only have put Mark and the big stranger's efforts in jeopardy. He had also probably saved them from a serious injury.

Unaware of the by-play at the other end of the wagon

[3] An occasion when Frank Derringer put the weapon concealed in his walking stick to use is told in: *COLD DECK, HOT LEAD.* J.T.E.

between its owner and the gambler, exerting still more of their combined gigantic strength, the blond giant and his helper were doing their utmost to carry out the marshal's instructions. Each had known the task would not be over when, or *if*, they contrived to elevate the vehicle to the required height. It would then have to be held there until the wheel could be replaced. They were equally aware that the replacing must be done at the earliest opportunity and on the first attempt. If they should be compelled to lower the enormous weight before the wheel was in position, they could not hope to regain sufficient of their expended energy to raise the wagon again.

At least, not before the parade arrived!

CHAPTER THREE

YOU CAN JUST BET YOUR LIFE I WOULD

Satisfied he could go ahead with the robbery in safety, Reg Wall bent over the pack. Just as he was about to start cutting open the tarpaulin cover, he learned he was in error with his assessment of the situation. The discovery was made via the toe of a boot meeting the seat of his breeches with considerable force. An agonised and profane exclamation was startled from him as, with the knife flying from his grasp, he was sent reeling to sprawl on hands and knees against the wall at the other side of the alley. Letting out another furious obscenity, he twisted himself around to sit on his aching rump and his right hand dipped towards the Navy Colt.

The weapon was not drawn!

In fact, Wall snatched his fingers away as if its butt was red hot!

Some people might have wondered why the movement was brought to such an end!

As far as outwards appearances went, the person who had delivered the kick did not seem particularly dangerous in spite of the weapons he was wearing.

Black haired, around six foot tall, with a slender build which nevertheless somehow implied it possessed the resilient strength of a steel spring, the man at whom Wall was glaring – much as a rabbit might at a coiled diamondback rattlesnake – looked as if he had not long entered his 'teens. There was an aura of almost babyish innocence about his Indian dark and handsome face; except for the eyes, that is. They were of a curious red hazel hue and held a glint which gave warning that the suggestion of youth and innocence was almost certainly deceptive. Dressed in the general fashion of a cowhand from Texas, the most noticeable difference being that his boots had low heels, his attire could not be described as gaudy. Rather the opposite, in fact. Each item, from the headgear through a tight rolled bandana, open necked shirt and pants to his footwear, was coloured black. So was the well designed weapon belt which supported in a low cavalry-twist holster on its right side an old walnut handled Colt Model of 1848 revolver with the butt turned forward. At the left hung an enormous ivory hilted James Black bowie knife.

There might be people in Mulrooney who would have regarded such armament, particularly in view of its archaic nature, as no more than the affectation of a youngster trying to impress his elders with a pretended toughness.

Wall could not be included in such a category.

Even though the pickpocket had only recently arrived in the town, he had spent sufficient time west of the Mississippi River to have learned that the Ysabel Kid had no need to make a *pretence* at being tough. All Wall had heard and seen informed him that there were, in fact, few men in the West – or elsewhere for that matter – who could exceed the baby-faced young Texan as far as that particular quality was concerned. Nor was his effectiveness as a fighting *man* reduced to any significant degree by his insistence upon retaining two weapons which many considered to be old fashioned and out of date.[1]

Certainly Wall did not believe this to be the case!

There was another factor which the pickpocket was taking into account. At that moment, it transcended considerations of his black-dressed assailant's potential as a very competent fighting man. Although he was not displaying a badge of office, like Mark Counter, he had served as a deputy town marshal under Dusty Fog. This implied he could have knowledge that Wall would have preferred to remain a secret.

The Kid's former official status was anything but a palatable thought for Wall. While he had been prevented from committing one crime, by cutting open the pack and removing some of its contents, he still had upon his person the silk handkerchief and expensive pocketbook acquired from the man in the crowd. Should the question of their

[1] For the benefit of new readers: details of the Ysabel Kid's background and special qualifications can be found in *APPENDIX THREE.* J.T.E.

ownership arise, each was so readily identifiable by his victim that they would provide undeniable proof of his guilt. Nor would the young Texan's retirement from office prevent him from raising the matter, having been made suspicious by Wall's actions.

'W-What did you do that for, mister?' the pickpocket croaked, adopting an air of injured innocence such as had on occasion earned him the sympathy of young and inexperienced peace officers, to their later embarrassment and mortification.

'Well now,' the Indian dark Texan replied, his pleasant tenor drawl underlaid with a timbre of chilled steel and his demeanour showing no discernible sympathy. 'I was sort of concluding on asking you-all what you reckoned you was up to.'

'I – I – !' Wall gulped, thinking fast in the hope of producing a convincing excuse for his behaviour as he concluded he was having no success in eliciting any favourable emotion from his present interrogator. Inspiration of a kind came and he hopefully converted it into words. 'I saw that pack lying there and was trying to find out who it belonged to.'

'And did you?' the Kid inquired, with such deceptive mildness that a chance onlooker might have been led to assume he believed what he was told.

'No,' Wall answered, suffering from no such illusions and wondering how he might give his actions a passable motive. 'There wasn't nothing to say on the outside.'

'So, being a real law abiding 'n' helpful visitor to this here fair community, you-all concluded to open her up and see if the owner'd left his name and address inside?' the Kid guessed. 'Mind you, though, there's some's'd maybe say it's not a whole heap likely's he would've.'

'Folks do mighty strange things sometime,' Wall pointed out, unable to decide whether the Texan was serious or not.

'Why sure, I was just thinking the same lil ole thing when I saw what you-all was doing,' the Kid replied, stepping forward and picking up the skinning knife. If he noticed the alarm which came to its owner's face as he returned it in an underhand flipping motion, he showed no sign of contrition over having been the cause. 'Anyways, *hombre*, there's no call for you to be taking so much fuss 'n' bother to find out. I *know* who it belongs to.'

'Y-You *do*?' Wall gasped, having bounced hurriedly aside as the knife landed in between his spread apart legs and making sure he made no gesture which could be construed as an attempt to pick it up.

'Would I *lie*?' the Kid challenged, with what might have passed as mildness although it did not impress the pickpocket in such a fashion. He gave an immediate, vehement negative shake of his head. 'Which being, happen you-all *wasn't* leaving town *real* soon, he'd likely want to come by *Ma Pinker's* place 'n' say, "Why thank you 'most to death", personal-like for thinking so friendly about helping him.'

'I'm not leav – !' Wall commenced, alarmed by the discovery that his interrogator knew where he was living.

'Now dog-my-cats if I just hadn't got took with the notion you-all *would* be,' the Kid interrupted, walking across the alley in a manner that was almost feline in its suggestion of latent and deadly menace. His face, as he came to a halt about six foot from the even more disconcerted pickpocket, had lost its aura of babyish innocence and become the coldly deadly mask more suited to one of his *Pehnane* Comanche ancestors. ' 'Cause, happen you *haven't* left next time I see you-all, I'm just natural' going to have to ask why not.'

'Wha – ?' Wall gurgled, having difficulty in following the Texan's exact meaning despite sensing it implied a serious threat to his well being.

'It's this way, *hombre*,' the Kid explained, his tone sardonic. 'We've heard tell about you-all 'n' the friendly-like ways you help yourself to others folks' belongings. Only, so far, we've not caught nor heard about you being at it here in town.' He lifted his left hand in a prohibitive gesture, leaving the right dangling with apparent negligence close to the forward turned butt of the old Dragoon Colt, as the pickpocket seemed on the point of injecting a comment. 'Sure, I *know* you hadn't cut into that big *hombre's* pack to take nothing out and I'm so trusting in your honesty that I'll take it you didn't aim to. But that don't change spit about you hauling your butt out of town.'

'Why?' Wall ventured to inquire.

'It's Cap'n Fog, see,' the Kid obliged. 'He's a man's likes things all neat 'n' tidy and, way he takes on when things aren't to his wantings, why life just ain't fit for living around him until he gets 'em's he wants. So he'll not be wanting no unfinished chores like *you-all* around after we've pulled out to make Marshal Kail Beauregard reckon's how we'n's've been neglectful of our legal' appointed duties. And what Cap'n Dusty don't want, being all for quiet 'an' peaceable living, I'm just mortal bound to see he gets it. *Understand?*'

'I understand,' Wall confirmed sullenly, having caught the gist of the lengthy and occasionally puzzling explanation.

'Wouldn't want you-all to get the notion I'm pushing you, like Injuns running a herd of buffalo over a cliff to get the meat the easy way,' the Kid went on. 'Just so long's you're gone on the evening train *tonight* will suit me fine. How about you?'

'Sure,' the pickpocket lied, although he had every intention of doing as he was ordered and, no matter how it was worded, an *order* the ultimatum had been. 'I'll be on the evening train.'

'*Bueno*,' the Kid assented. 'Now get up, so's I can make sure you've *not* been helping yourself to some of those good tax-paying citizens' possibles while you was on your way here.'

'I haven't!' Wall prevaricated, obeying the command to rise reluctantly and hoping his consternation over the prospect of being searched did not show.

'And *I'm* from Missouri,' the Kid countered. 'I've just natural' got to be shown.'

However, before the Indian-dark young Texan could adhere to the alleged proclivity of people from the State of Missouri by insisting upon proof by visible evidence, a change in the background sounds diverted his attention.

Seeing what was likely to be the only opportunity he would be presented, Wall took advantage of it the moment his interrogator looked away. Displaying a facility an eel might have envied, he twisted away from where he had been standing pressed against the wall and darted along the alley as fast as his legs would carry him. He gave no thought to the skinning knife he was leaving behind, being more concerned with the possibility of pursuit or – infinitely worse – receiving a .44 calibre bullet from the ancient, but still *very* lethal Dragoon Colt which was hanging so readily available on the Kid's gunbelt.

Reaching the end of the alley without either eventuality occurring, the pickpocket swerved behind the saloon and kept going. A glance to his rear showed he was not being followed and he slowed to a walk. In spite of having been permitted to escape, however, he had no intention of remaining in Mulrooney. Unfortunately, there was one problem presented by such an unanticipated departure. Because of a run of bad luck in his gambling recently, even with the couple of items of loot he had acquired, he still lacked sufficient funds to leave by the evening train.

There was, Wall concluded, only one solution!

Another victim must be found and robbed!

Despite hearing the pickpocket's hurried departure, whereupon he turned and twisted the Dragoon from its holster, the Kid neither bothered to give chase nor fire. Among the many other things he had learned during his years of association with Dusty Fog was to have a slightly higher appreciation of the sanctity of human life than had been instilled during his formative years as a member of the *Pehnane* band of the Comanche nation[2] Aware that to shoot down a fleeing criminal – who had at most purloined a few objects of no exceptional value – would not be countenanced by his *amigo* and leader, nor the new incumbent to the office of town marshal, he refrained. Nor, knowing where Wall could be found if necessary, did he bother to give chase.

Neither idleness nor a cowhand's antipathy towards carrying out any form of strenuous activity while on foot, unless it was absolutely necessary, had caused the Kid to decide against going after the pickpocket. Not only did he want to find out how Mark Counter was faring, he could envisage a possible benefit which might accrue from allowing Wall to escape unimpeded. Unless the miscreant chose some other means, which the Kid considered unlikely, his departure from Mulrooney would be delayed until the arrival of the evening train. Should any of the crowd have suffered from Wall's depredations, they were sure to have discovered and

[2] Details of the Ysabel Kid's formative years are given in: *COMANCHE*. J.T.E.

reported the loss before then. So, supplied with the requisite information, Beauregard's standing in the community would be enhanced by the rapidity with which he located and arrested the culprit.

Returning the Dragoon to its holster, the Kid picked up the skinning knife and eyed it with disdain as he mentally compared its qualities with those of the big bowie knife he carried. Then he turned his gaze to the pack. Considering its owner had been incautious in leaving it unattended and unwatched, no matter how good the reason, he decided to take it with him as he rejoined his friends on the street.

'Whooee!' the Indian dark young Texan ejaculated, as he felt the weight of the pack on starting to lift it. 'I wish that short-grown, sneaky son-of-a-bitch'd tried to tote it off, what it'd've been like' to do to him should he have. Happen that big jasper carried it far, he must be close to's strong as Mark.'

* * * * *

'Excuse me, young man. But were those two – gentlemen – proposing to let you buy something of value?'

On being greeted with such a question – spoken in a feminine voice that had an accent redolent of a well-educated Southerner upbringing – as he was entering the waiting room of the railroad depot, the blond haired young Texan looked around for the speaker. The tone was somewhat harsh and imperious, reminding him of the only female schoolteacher with whom he had had any contact. Nor did his first sight of the person who had addressed him cause him to revise his opinion that she might indeed earn a living as a schoolteacher.

Perhaps five foot eight in height, the woman who was the room's only other occupant would hardly have been classed as attractive or desirable even by a man who had long been deprived of feminine company. A 'spoon bonnet' which resembled and was roughly the same off-yellow colour as a well weathered canopy for a Conestoga wagon, devoid of the decorations usually employed to brighten such headgear, entirely concealed her hair. Her sombre and severe black travelling costume was just as effective in preventing any indication of the contours it concealed, other than suggesting they could be more bulky than curvaceous. Whatever good looks nature might have endowed on her were spoiled by a pair of large, horn rimmed spectacles and a set of sallow features with a somewhat bulbous nose. She was grasping a black umbrella of considerable proportions in her right hand, which – as in the case of its mate – was gloved and concealed all evidence of her marital status. The left hand gripped the neck of an equally bulky and shapeless old reticule. There was also a decrepit looking carpetbag at her feet.

'Well now, ma'am,' the youngster answered, snatching off his hat in what appeared to be an involuntary gesture, apparently too surprised by the inquiry to notice the absence of the man he had claimed he was going to meet. 'I don't rightly reckon's how I know what you-all mean.'

'Come now!' the woman snapped, reminding the blond even more of the schoolmistress from his not too long departed days as a pupil. She reminded him of those far from infrequent occasions when he was being called to account for some piece of misbehaviour. 'You know perfectly well what I mean!'

'Well now, ma'am,' the Texan said, shuffling his feet and spinning the hat between his hands involuntarily, wishing he felt less like an errant schoolboy. 'Could be I do at that – Only I don't – '

'Only you don't see just what the Sam Hill it has to do with an interfering old busybody like *me*,' the woman suggested, as the almost truculent words trailed to an inconclusive halt.

'I wouldn't go so far as say *that*, ma'am,' the Texan protested, despite some such sentiment having occurred to him.

'And why *not*?' the woman challenged in an authoritative manner. 'Because that's what you were thinking.'

'Maybe so, ma'am,' the youngster answered evasively and with none of the brashness he had employed while talking to the Easterner and Mexican. 'Thing being – '

'You're wondering how I guessed what they were up to?' the woman prompted, as the youngster's comment was once again ended without being completed.

'Something like that,' the blond admitted, after a moment and with just a hint of defiance.

'It so happens I chanced to overhear them talking on the train shortly before it pulled into the depot,' the woman began to explain, but was not granted the opportunity to continue.

'And you're figuring on cutting in on the deal?' the Texan hinted.

'I most assuredly am *not*!' the woman snapped indignantly. 'And I would strongly advise that you also refrain from having any dealings with them.'

'Why's that, ma'am?'

'Have you any knowledge of precious stones?'

'Only that they're worth a whole pile of money and the gals surely do like them.'

'Is that all you know?'

'Well, now, ma'am,' the Texan asserted, with the pompous air of one who wished to prove he was an experienced man of the world. 'My folks didn't raise them no stupid kids and I reckon I know something good when I see it.'

'I'm pleased to hear it,' the woman remarked drily. 'And, of course, you can tell when a – diamond, shall we say – is genuine?'

'I've allus heard a real 'n'all slice glass like a hot knife going through bear tallow,' the Texan declared.

'It has that quality,' the woman conceded, still with a sardonic aura. 'And, naturally, should you be offered one or more for sale, you would sure to subject them to such a test before buying them?'

'You can just bet your life I would, ma'am!' the blond youngster stated.

'And have you already done so?' the woman inquired.

'Well no, ma'am,' the Texan confessed. 'But Mr Rickmansworth allows to be a jewellery drummer, or some such, from back East and knows all about 'em. *He* allows they're worth buying 'specially when they come's cheap as we've been asked.'

'I'm sure he possesses sufficient knowledge to make such a claim,' the woman replied. 'On the other hand, I think you might be advised to ask for a second opinion before you make any purchase.'

'I'll keep it in mind, ma'am,' the youngster promised. 'Only, even if Mr Rickmansworth isn't what he claims to be,

I reckon I'm way too slick to be hornswoggled by any greaser.'

'I hope you're right,' the woman answered, then gave a shrug indicating she was washing her hands of the affair. 'Well, anyway, I've warned you. What you decide now is entirely up to you.'

'Yes, ma'am,' the Texan agreed. 'I reckon it is at that.'

CHAPTER FOUR

IT'S WHAT I'M BEST AT

Despite hearing the band striking up as an indication that the Grand Parade was soon to be starting, Mark Counter and his helper watched Marshal Kail Beauregard's signals. For his part, the peace officer did not attempt to hurry things up. When he signified the vehicle was high enough, the two big men braced themselves for the final and most gruelling effort required to keep the vehicle steady while its wheel was being replaced.

A silence that could almost be felt descended over the onlookers as the other two men began to manoeuvre the wheel into place. While the pair were aware of the urgent need to work as quickly as possible, each also appreciated that too much haste might cause them to fumble and produce a delay which could bring the lifters' efforts to nothing. Watching and moving with extreme care, they eased the hole in the centre of the hub until the tip of the axle was directly behind it. Then, hardly daring to breathe in case something should go wrong at that late stage, they began to work the wheel along the shaft.

There was a concerted letting out of mutually held back breath from the spectators, echoed by sighs of relief from the men handling the wheel as they watched the tip of the axle emerging. When the wheel would go no further, one of them nodded to Beauregard.

Although they were informed of the situation, the blond giant and his massive assistant did not relax immediately. Instead, they allowed the enormous weight to settle slowly and under control. Not until assured that all was holding satisfactorily did they remove their hands from beneath the bed of the wagon. Leaning against the tailgate, breathing in great gulps of air, with perspiration soaking their faces and torsoes they showed just how mighty a strain they had undergone. Looking at each other, neither was at first able to say a word. Instead, they exchanged grins redolent of satisfaction in a difficult and arduous task well done.

'Where's the wheel nut?' Beauregard shouted, the moment the two men had completed the replacement, glancing towards the corner around which the first members of the band leading the parade were appearing.

'Right here, marshal!' announced the helper who had retrieved the nut, advancing and starting to replace it as soon as the lifters released their hold.

'Get on the box ready to pull out, Mr Walton!' Beauregard ordered, deciding to content himself with having the nut tightened by hand instead of taking the time to obtain a suitable spanner from the tool box attached to the side of the wagon.

'Sure,' the businessman answered, obeying and trying to conceal his disappointment.

'All right, Mr Walton,' the marshal continued, when the man tightening the nut stepped aside and nodded. 'Take it down the alley over there as quickly as you can, please.'

In the opinion of Frank Derringer, who was cognisant of the situation and its implications, the peace officer's last word was a fortunate, or inspired, inclusion. Its use indicated that, despite having been faced with a crisis over which a loss of temper would have been excusable, he still retained the courtesy to make a polite request of the person who was responsible for the whole situation.

Scowling malevolently rather than duplicating the elation being displayed by the onlookers, Walton began to do as he was instructed. Gathering up the reins and preparing to shove off the brake with his boot, he wondered how he could cause a further delay. Almost immediately, he was struck by an appreciation of how undesirable such an action would be. To delay now would cause all the recriminations which would ensue to fall where they rightfully belonged, on his head.

A secondary impulse, to pretend to have misunderstood the marshal's directions and continue along the street towards the approaching parade, was discarded with an equal alacrity, and not only because he feared the recriminations of the crowd. There were two even more potent reasons for refraining.

On hearing Beauregard's instructions, Derringer had moved aside. However, he was still watching in a coldly threatening manner and was clearly ready to cope with any further attempts at treachery.

If *that* was not enough, the businessman noticed an even more disturbing factor had made its appearance.

Glancing around in search of inspiration, Walton saw the Ysabel Kid emerging from the alley alongside Henry's Saloon. Despite being hampered by a large, obviously heavy pack which he was dragging in his right hand and a skinning knife he was grasping in his other fist, he could easily relieve himself of both by opening his hands should he see the need for such an action.

Walton did not doubt the Indian-dark young Texan would consider such a need existed if he shared the gambler's suspicions. What was more, while Derringer's response to further attempts at humiliating or causing embarrassment for the marshal might be tempered by concern for the susceptibilities of less well informed onlookers, the Kid was less likely to harbour such qualms. As he had demonstrated frequently prior to and during his period of office as a deputy marshal in the town, he was no respecter of public opinion even if flouting it might lead to criticism of his behaviour. Perhaps he would not go to extremes as he had on one occasion when he had heard a woman give orders that Dusty Fog's throat was to be cut and his ears brought to her. The Kid had overheard the message and had returned the would-be assassin to her in the same fashion.[1] But the businessman was disinclined to chance invoking whatever repercussions might ensure if he continued to delay the parade.

Yielding to the inevitable, with ill concealed bad grace, Walton set the team into motion. As he went in the direction indicated by Beauregard, he decided that an early absence from town – with pressing business elsewhere as an excuse – might be in order. Guiding the wagon down the alley, he

[1] The incident is described in: *A TOWN CALLED YELLOWDOG.* J.T.E.

kept going towards his freight yard so he could make the necessary preparations to leave.

Feeling their support was no longer needed as the wagon set off, Mark and the bearded man transferred themselves to the subsidy offered by the hitching rail in front of Henry's Saloon. The spectators obligingly made space for them as they ducked underneath it. Then, still breathing hard although giving no other sign of having suffered any ill effects from performing their Herculean feat of strength, they nodded in response to the congratulations being offered on all sides.

'*Gracias*, Mark, friend,' the marshal said, joining the two big men and there was no doubting the sincerity with which he spoke.

'*Es nada, amigo,*' the blond giant replied, straightening up and flexing his aching muscles gingerly.

'Allus right happy to help with a mite of lifting or toting, Marshal,' the burly newcomer went on. 'Seeing's how doing it don't call for no thinking, it's what I'm best at I've allus been told.'

'I've never seen such done better,' Beauregard declared in tones of admiration. 'Only I don't reckon either of you-all would want to do it *too* regular.'

'Not more than once a month and only then happen it's got no more than *twenty-nine* days in it,' Mark stated. 'Which doing it just this once's sure as hell made me thirsty.'

'And me,' the bearded giant seconded.

'Here, dry off on this and put your shirt on, Mark,' suggested the plump and jovial featured owner of the saloon, having collected a couple of towels and offering them to the two big men. 'Then come on in, both of you. I've got a right smart cure for being thirsty.'

'Well now, I'd surely admire to sink me a schooner of cold beer,' the newcomer admitted, his voice sleepily gentle, then he glanced along the street. 'But I'd like to see the parade go by first, happen it's all the same with you. We don't *never* get to see nothing so fancy out where I hail from.'

'That's fine with me,' Mark assented, rubbing his torso with the towel. 'We'll take you-all up on that offer after the parade, Henry.'

Inspired by the knowledge of the occasion's importance

and the enthusiastic response from the assembled populace, the band was playing with great gusto as they strode along the street. The noise they were making prevented even the keen ears of the Kid from hearing the crackle of gunfire in the vicinity of the railroad depot.

* * * * *

'God-damn it, Julie!' Juan Jose 'Spanish' Cervantes protested, peering around the corner behind which he had once more retired, after almost five minutes had elapsed without the blond haired young Texan having returned. 'Either the bastard's got suspicious, or he's been talked out of it. He's not coming back.'

'Your trouble, "Spanish", is you're always too impatient,' countered the man who had introduced himself as 'Julian Rickmansworth' to the intended victim of his and his partner's version of the 'diamond switch' confidence trick, although he too was growing worried by the cowhand's continued absence. 'He took the bait like a largemouth bass sucking down a nightcrawler.'

'Then where *is* he?' the 'Mexican' challenged. 'I don't recollect seeing no god-damned rancher talking to somebody at the depot when we got off the train. Nor *anybody* at all, except that woman who come in with us, comes to that.'

'There were some men in the waiting room at the other side of the tracks, which is where he said he was going,' Rickmansworth corrected, having looked around in the hope of locating a potential 'mark' upon whom to commence operations after the train on which they had arrived had pulled out. 'And, as the shipping pens are across there, that's where any such business would be transacted. Anyway, you'd better keep out of sight. Even such a smart-assed, know-it-all, son-of-a-bitch as he *thinks* he is would smell a rat if he saw you're still hanging around.'

'All right, have it *your* way!' Cervantes sniffed. 'Only I still say we won't see hide nor hair of him again.'

An annoyed snort broke from Rickmansworth as he watched his partner's head disappear behind the corner of the closed general store at the opposite end to where they had accosted the young Texan. Then he swung his gaze to the railroad depot. Possessing complete faith in his competency in their illicit field (although he was puzzled over the delay which had provoked 'Spanish's' protest) he was more satisfied than surprised some thirty seconds later to see the blond strolling from the waiting room. As he had anticipated, not only was the cowhand returning, but was also coming alone as promised. He had felt sure anyone so callow and arrogant, having a desire to be taken for an experienced man of the world in spite of his youth, would do nothing to jeopardise a chance to achieve this ambition and become rich.

Although having confidence in his shrewd assessment of human nature, the Easterner nevertheless scanned the depot building from which the Texan appeared to make sure nobody was watching. There were four windows and a door in the wall at which Rickmansworth was looking. While the windows on either side of the waiting room's entrance were clean enough to offer a point of vantage, the other two were situated in what he knew to be the male and female rest-rooms. To ensure the privacy of those who availed themselves of the latter's facilities, the panes of their windows had been covered with black paint and rendered opaque.

While the view into the waiting room was restricted, the Easterner decided he and the Texan were not under observation. Because of the festivities elsewhere in the town, there had been none of the usual crowd that would otherwise have congregated at the depot. Even the two railroad officials brought there by necessity had not delayed their departure once the formalities of the train's arrival had been completed. The only other passenger to disembark had been the somewhat formidable-looking woman to whom 'Spanish' had referred and she was nowhere to be seen.

Satisfied that everything was progressing as required, Rickmansworth waited with pleasurable anticipation to carry on into the next stage of the confidence trick.

'Ah, here you are at last, young man,' the Easterner greeted. Seeking to discover the reason for the delay, so as to decide whether it might constitute a threat, he went on, 'I thought perhaps you had changed your mind and lost your desire to purchase a share of the diamonds.'

'You-all don't have one tiny lil ole chance of *that* coming off, mister,' the Texan asserted, dipping his left hand into the near side hip pocket of his Levi's pants. 'I'd've come back sooner, only the boss was squatting on the pot with the "squitters" in the backhouse. Way he was a-squirting it out, you'd've thought he'd been guzzling croton oil[2] like it was whisky all night.'

'Quite!' Rickmansworth put in hastily and, having a fastidious nature which revolted against such crude comments, he needed to exert all his willpower to refrain from expressing his distaste still further.

'Anyways,' the Texan continued, making no attempt to conceal his amusement over the reaction his remark had elicited from the pompous-looking Easterner, 'he got through in the end, wiped his butt on that old corncob – or whatever they use in there – and gave me my money.'

'You didn't mention why you wanted it, did you?' Rickmansworth asked, controlling his revulsion and darting a covetous glance at the wad of what appeared to be five dollar bills which the intended victim was bringing into view. Darting another look to the waiting room and ensuring that nobody had arrived to watch the youngster, he commenced, 'Because – !'

'I said's I *wouldn't*, didn't I just?' the blond snapped with asperity, tucking the money into the pocket on the left side of his calfskin vest. Extending the hand he had emptied, he demanded rather than asked, 'I'll have me another look at the four I'll be taking, happen that's all right with you.'

'Of course it is,' Rickmansworth assented, exuding a spurious amiability and refraining from showing the slight trepidation he was experiencing over the request. Although he had placed the pouch obtained from the 'Mexican' in his jacket's right hand pocket on 'purchasing' it, confident that his partner would be able to prevent any attempt to acquire the contents without payment being made, the pouch he now removed came from the other side. Tipping four of the stones into the proffered palm, he went on, 'Here you are, young man. Beautiful things, aren't they?'

'They surely do look pretty, kind of like lumps of broken glass, only shinier,' the Texan commented. If he attached any

[2] 'Croton oil' : a pale yellow, or yellowish-brown viscid oil obtained from a small East Indian tree, *Croton Tiglium*, for use as a purgative and rubefacient. J.T.E.

significance to the speed with which the Easterner's left hand returned the pouch to the pocket and went to grasp the centre of the walking stick as he completed the description, he made no reference to it. Instead, he glanced at the nearby window of the store and drawled, 'Talking of *glass*, I've allus heard tell's how a diamond'll cut it real easy. So, being's how I've allus been one for wanting to see things I've never yet seen, damned if I don't reckon's how I'll give these lil beauties here a whirl at it.'

'How?' Rickmansworth inquired, hard put to conceal his consternation over the possibility of such an experiment being conducted. 'You don't have any glass.'

'There's all I'll need right here in this window, though,' the Texan pointed out, indicating the object in question with a brief motion of his right thumb.

'But you'll *cut* it!' the Easterner objected, before he could prevent what he belatedly realised was the wrong response and wishing unavailingly he had claimed the information was incorrect.

'Not so all-fired much,' the Texan answered, in a determined tone. 'I'm only fixing to make an itty-bitty nick on a corner, not slice all the way down the son-of-a-bitching window from top to bottom.'

Frowning and opening his mouth to make a spurious protest against the damage to private property, no matter how small it might be, Rickmansworth closed it with the words unsaid. Showing clearly that no amount of argument would cause him to change his mind, the youngster was already stepping to the window.

That the Easterner refrained from protesting did not indicate that he had conceded the Texan had the right to conduct the test.

Just the opposite was the case!

The last thing the distinguished-looking 'confidence man' wanted was for such an experiment to take place.

As a precaution against a prospective victim possessing knowledge of such precious stones, or being sufficiently lacking in trust as to insist upon those which were offered being examined and valued by an independent jeweller, the pouch Cervantes had handed to the Texan contained genuine diamonds. However, it had not been from this one that

Rickmansworth delivered the four pieces which the youngster was about to subject to the glass-cutting test.

When the Easterner had suggested that the Texan should be their first 'mark' in Mulrooney, neither he nor Cervantes had thought to deviate from the routine which they had employed for a number of years throughout numerous cities and towns east of the Mississippi River. They had been so convinced that the blond youngster would fall into their clutches, that it had never occurred to either of them to have the 'Mexican' use the other genuine stones he was carrying as was their practice when contending with older, more cautious men.

Nor, up to that moment, had Rickmansworth experienced the slightest qualms over following their tried-and-true method of operation. He had considered the confidence trick was progressing, if anything, more smoothly than had been the case on many other occasions. Because the 'mark' had appeared to have accepted his declaration on the authenticity of the stones, he had used four from the substitute bag in the belief that they would be taken and paid for without question.

Being all too aware of what the result of the experiment would be, the Easterner doubted whether the situation could be settled amicably. His instincts warned him that a person with the young Texan's arrogant temperament would be unlikely to accept that he too had been duped by the 'Mexican'. So he tightened his right hand's grip on the silver knob of the walking stick and his left made a slight twisting motion.

'Well now, will you-all just take a peek at *that*!' the Texan suggested, having run one of the 'diamonds' across the lower corner of the window's bottom pane without it having any effect upon the glass. Although he did not look around as he was speaking, there was a growing timbre of suspicion in his tone. 'Could it be I've heard wrong?'

'The test isn't conclusive, young man,' Rickmansworth replied, hoping the situation could be resolved without the need for violence. 'On occasion, one comes across a diamond which won't cut glass.'

'Do tell,' the Texan drawled, still standing with his back to the 'confidence man'. 'And there I was starting to wonder if maybe these here aren't the same doohickies I looked at afore. Anyways, I'll just try the others and see how they stack up. That way I'll know for sure whether I'm getting flim-flammed or not.'

A malevolent scowl distorted the Easterner's distinguished features, rendering their expression more in keeping with his true nature. Carrying out the 'diamond switch' confidence trick required a fair amount of working capital. In addition to the cost of purchasing the medallion which was always the first object supposedly offered for sale by the 'Mexican', the genuine stones and their identical, if less valuable replicas, there were other expenses. These included the clothes needed by Rickmansworth for his pose as a wealthy businessman, plus the charges for travelling upon those sections of trains in which potential victims could be found, and occupying rooms at hotels of a similarly high class.

So, having a considerable sum of money invested in their latest foray, the Easterner was disinclined to let anything – or *anybody*, particularly a person he regarded as being an obnoxious and offensive small town hick – put the confidence trick in danger of exposure before at least a portion of the money he and his partner had already expended was recovered.

Certainly such a state of affairs was not to be permitted when the threat to it could be removed permanently, without any especial difficulty and, considering the wad of money the Texan had displayed, profitably.

Peering surreptitiously around the corner of the store, Cervantes had watched the way in which the situation was developing. Realising that things were not going as planned, he considered it was advisable to allow his partner to deal with the blond youngster. Although there was considerable noise from a band in the background, which he deduced was leading a parade as part of the Independence Day festivities, he preferred to avoid the chance of attracting unwanted attention by drawing and firing even one shot from his revolver. There was, in his judgement, a sound reason for the decision. Unless their prospective victim was lying, which seemed unlikely as he had returned with the money he had claimed he was fetching, he had companions close by. In spite of the noise on the other street, they were almost certain to hear the shot and come to investigate.

On the other hand, Rickmansworth had a means of silencing the youngster which was as efficacious as a bullet and far more silent. Twice during their association, the 'Mexican' had seen his partner demonstrate an ability to kill without permitting either victim an opportunity to resist or raise an outcry. The fact that he was making preparations to do so on this occasion suggested he was confident he would not have been seen by the Texan's companions.

Throwing another searching glance at the waiting room, still without locating anything to suggest there were witnesses other than his partner to see what he was intending to do, Rickmansworth gave another twist and tugged sharply at the stick with his left hand. The wooden section slid away immediately. Its removal exposed the spear-pointed and razor sharp steel blade of the sword which formed its secondary, or – at that moment – primary function. Retaining the sheath in his left hand, he stepped forward on tiptoe and, directing the point towards his unsuspecting victim's back, went into an almost classic fencer's lunge.

The attack was launched with swift and deadly precision!

It appeared certain to achieve its lethal purpose!

CHAPTER FIVE

YOU'LL WANT *ME* TO PERSUADE HIM

There was only one snag in the path of Julian Rickmansworth's murderous scheme.

The prospective victim, who had been playing a part as adeptly as either of the 'confidence men', was far from being as unsuspecting as his would-be killer imagined.

So, even as the Easterner became aware that his purpose had been discerned, the discovery came just too late for him to profit by it.

Having harboured suspicions that he might be contending with a pair of conspirators intending to bilk him, even before he had received the suggestions from the woman in the waiting room, the youngster had not been unaware of the possible danger if he continued to negotiate with them. What was more, having seen similar devices, he had suspected Rickmansworth's walking stick might hold a concealed and deadly weapon. So, while he was carrying out the test to prove his suspicions, he had also been keeping the Easterner under observation via the reflections in the store's window. The moment he had seen the blade unsheathed, he had known he was not doing the two men an injustice by doubting their credibility. Furthermore, he had decided how he could best protect himself.

Spinning around while taking a very hurried side-step, the Texan whipped his left arm inwards so the back of his hand swung and deflected the swiftly approaching blade before it could reach its intended target. At the same time, working in perfect co-ordination, he bunched and threw a blow with his right fist. The hard knuckles caught the side of Rickmansworth's jaw, arriving with a force that precipitated him in a twirling sprawl away from his proposed victim. Losing his hold on the sword and its wooden sheath as he went, he was unable to prevent himself toppling headlong to the ground half-way across the street.

Seeing his partner's failure, Juan Cervantes let out a snarl of annoyance and anger. It was obvious to him that he must now intervene, and he concluded there was only one way in which he could do so – by using his gun, regardless of whether he would incur undesirable and in all probability hostile attentions when he fired.

Stepping from his place of concealment, Cervantes suddenly began to appreciate that his task was not a sinecure. While he had drawn the Freeman Army revolver on realising the scheme might be going wrong, he had failed to take the precaution of cocking its hammer. It was an omission which no gun fighter trained west of the Mississippi River would have contemplated, but he lacked such technical knowledge. Although he had been carrying the weapon as an aid to establishing his character as a Mexican of dubious background since he and Rickmansworth had arrived in Kansas three weeks earlier, he had never needed – nor even taken the trouble – to fire it. He had handled firearms in the past and had used one to kill a 'mark' who detected the exchange of the pouches being made, but that had been at such close quarters it was impossible for him to have missed and no skill in aiming was required.

Taking warning from the speed with which the Texan had moved to deal with his partner, Cervantes decided against trying to go closer. Halting just clear of the corner, he fetched the hammer to fully cocked and began to raise the revolver to shoulder height. As he was starting to take aim at the Texan, he was made forcibly and unpleasantly aware that his partner had been in error and there was at least one witness to what was taking place.

'Behind you!' shrieked a feminine voice, from somewhere inside the railroad depot's waiting room.

However, events were proving that the warning was not needed.

Once again, even before the precautionary words were uttered, the Texan was displaying an awareness of the impending danger which seemed remarkably well developed for one of his youth.

Although the blond had not heard the clicking of Cervantes's revolver being cocked, because of the noise of the parade along Trail Street, he had anticipated some such action might be taken against him. So, having avoided being impaled by the sword of his first would-be killer, he was already starting to face the point from which he surmised, correctly, that the second threat would originate. The woman's words confirmed his suspicions.

For all the Texan's perception and rapid response, he was almost too late. As he was moving away from the window in a hurried bound, the 'Mexican's' weapon cracked.

By chance, rather than through deliberately applied skill, Cervantes's aim was good!

Too good, in fact, under the circumstances!

The .44 calibre bullet passed through where the blond's head had been an instant before. It was so close he felt the wind of its passing between the back of his neck and the stetson which, having been dislodged by the violence of his movements, was trailing behind him on its *barbiquejo* chin-strap.

Spluttering out obscenities in his native Spanish and English, Cervantes jerked back the revolver's hammer as soon as he realised he had missed. While he was operating it, he began to turn the barrel so it would once more be pointing at the already halting youngster.

Alighting from the bound which had saved his life, the Texan dipped his right hand with great alacrity to the stag-horn handle of the offside Army Colt. As he drew it, he was pulling back the hammer with his thumb. However, the action was not completed, nor did he insert his forefinger through the triggerguard until *after* the barrel was clear of the holster and was turned away from him.[1] While he went into a crouch on slightly flexed legs and spread apart feet, he made no attempt to elevate the weapon above waist level.

Like his assailant, the youngster appreciated that the distance separating them was not conducive to accuracy unless it was enforced by a careful employment of the sights. The difference was, being far more experienced in such matters, he accepted time would not allow him to do so. Furthermore,

[1] For the benefit of new readers: an example of how dangerous a failure to take this precaution could be is given in: *THE FAST GUN*. J.T.E.

he had at his disposal a method of shooting by which a hit might be obtained. Even if it failed to achieve its primary purpose, he knew the means offered something almost as useful.

Locking his right elbow tightly against his side, the Texan pointed the Colt by instinctive alignment. Having depressed the trigger, he only needed to release the hammer to discharge the uppermost bullet in the cylinder. Having done so, however, he retained the trigger in the firing position instead of allowing it to go forward. Without waiting to see whether his shot had had any effect, bringing his left arm across in a circular motion, he used the heel of his hand to pull back and release the hammer instead of using his right thumb again. This allowed the second shot to follow *very* closely on the heels of the first.

Although the white smoke from Cervantes's own weapon had not created any problem, being wafted behind him by the gentle breeze, Cervantes found the same did not apply to the larger double cloud produced by the Texan's Army Colt. It swirled before the crouching figure to such effect that the 'Mexican' had difficulty in taking aim. Alarmed by the sound of two closely passing bullets, he jerked at the trigger in the hope of preventing others from reaching him.

By continuing to 'fan' the hammer with his left hand, the youngster was able to discharge the remaining four bullets from his Colt in extremely rapid succession. Nor was he deterred from his efforts when lead from the 'Mexican's' gun came through the swirling powder smoke being emitted by his weapon. The second attempt to shoot him was even less successful than its predecessor, going by at a greater distance. The smoke was the added bonus offered by 'fanning', partially hiding him from his assailant.

By turning the barrel slightly between each shot, the youngster caused the bullets to fly on slightly – but significantly – divergent courses. Although the first three missed by a decreasing margin, the fourth and fifth took the 'Mexican' in the chest.[2] Either would have been fatal, the one on the

[2] Should any reader doubt that such accurate shooting is possible when 'fanning' the hammer, the author suggests corroboration can be obtained by reading Pages 96–102, *FAST AND FANCY REVOLVER SHOOTING AND POLICE TRAINING* by Ed McGivern. J.T.E.

left almost instantaneously so as it tore through his heart in passing. A screech of torment burst from him as, with the revolver spinning from his grasp, he was flung off his feet. He went crashing down in the sprawling and uncaring way of one who was on the verge of death.

Confident there was nothing further to fear from the 'Mexican', the youngster swung around. Drawing his left-hand Colt with an equal speed and facility while turning, he walked to where a dazed looking Rickmansworth was sitting up. Deftly returning the empty revolver to its holster, he brought its mate into line as the Easterner glared at him and reached beneath the left side of the now dirt-stained jacket.

'Whatever you-all've got under there'd better be let stay put, *hombre*,' the Texan warned, but without any of his previous bombast and arrogance, thumb-cocking the second Colt. 'Even *happen* I'd let you get it out and you shot me, the money you saw's nothing more than a couple of five dollar bills wrapped round some pieces of paper I got from the backhouse at the depot. Which's what took me so long afore I got back to you.'

'Y – you planned to cheat *me*?' Rickmansworth demanded, oozing genuine indignation.

'No more than you-all and your *amigo* come here aiming to do to folks,' the youngster pointed out. 'Only I was aiming to stop you doing it to them, not to take nothing from you.'

'I – I don't understand,' the Easterner admitted.

'The name's Waco, mister,' the Texan introduced. 'I'm not a deputy marshal any more, but I've heard tell a feller can make him a citizen's arrest should he find a couple of yahoos are figuring on flim-flamming him with the old "diamond switch".'[3]

Crouching at the window of the 'Ladies' restroom, which she had raised sufficiently to let her see through and shout the warning, the woman who had accosted the young Texan earlier had been able to hear what he and Rickmansworth were saying.

'So you're Waco, are you?' the onlooker mused, straightening up and closing the window as she concluded there would

[3] Details of how the 'diamond switch' could be operated successfully are given in: *CALAMITY, MARK AND BELLE*. J.T.E.

be no further need for action on her part. 'You had me fooled just now. And you're as good as I've heard.'

* * * * *

'Pardon me, sir,' said a polite voice, with an accent suggestive of Bostonian Back Bay origins. 'But could you inform us, peradventure, of the identity of that handsome blond giant who performed the prodigious feat of strength to which we were privy prior to the passing of yonder parade?'

Feeling a hand laid gently on his arm, as he was on the point of going into Henry's Saloon after having watched the marchers pass by, the Texas cowhand who had suggested how the wagon might be removed realised that the question was being directed at him. Turning, he studied the two people who confronted him with a mixture of interest and incredulity. There was, he concluded after subjecting them to a brief scrutiny, an excuse for what he considered to be – although he would not have expressed it in those exact words – an exhibition of abysmal ignorance.

Of medium height, middle aged, portly and in his middle forties, the man who had posed the question was well and expensively dressed. He had on a grey billycock hat, a brown three-piece suit clearly made to his measure, a white silk shirt, a multi-hued cravat of the same material and Hersome gaiter boots. The neck-wear was impaled by a stickpin with a fair-sized stone that could be a diamond, and a gold watch chain with a couple of impressive seals attached stretched across his ample mid-section as a further indication of prosperity. His plump, sun-reddened features had an expression of amiable inquiry and its lines were such as to inspire confidence in his good nature.

The woman at the speaker's side looked to be about half his age, but there was no facial or physical resemblance to suggest she might be his daughter. Red haired and beautiful, she was slightly taller than her companion. Clad in a Wave-lean hat and a dark blue tailored two-piece travelling costume, with a frilly bosomed white silk blouse sporting a decorously high neck, the garments showed off her curvaceous figure to its best advantage. She had a folded, dainty parasol in her left hand and a small vanity bag swung from wrist. She was well, if not over, jewelled; although ut a ring to indicate marital status. There was an ex- ession of eager appeal on her face which would have softened the heart of a far less susceptible person than the young cowhand.

'Why that was *Mark Counter*, ma'am, sir,' the Texan replied. 'He rides for the OD Connected's floating outfit and's Cap'n Dusty Fog's right bower.'[4]

'So *that's* who he is,' the Bostonian said, his tone implying he was impressed by the information. 'And does the equally Herculean gentleman whose participation greatly facilitated the successful outcome of Mr Counter's endeavours perchance appertain to the same illustrious association to which you refer?'

'Well now,' the cowhand answered, frowning in puzzlement, 'iffen all that fancy jaw-flapping means, "Does the big *hombre* with the beard ride for the OD Connected along of Mark?" the answer's closer to "no" than "yes".'

'Could you mayhap hazard an approximation as to the nature of his chosen field of endeavour in that case?' the portly man inquired.

'Huh?' the cowhand grunted, staring in blank lack of comprehension.

'What kind of work does he do?' the young woman explained.

'Looks to me like he might be a buffalo hunter, ma'am,' the cowhand declared, conceding there was an excuse for the pair's lack of knowledge regarding the way in which men in different types of employment tended to dress. The couple had clearly not been west of the Big Muddy for any great period. ' 'Cepting he's a whole heap cleaner'n most of that kind I've run across.'

'I yield without stint to your superior and more experienced point of view, sir,' the Bostonian asserted. 'But, from no matter what source the bearded gentleman attains his sustenance, they are still two most remarkably fine representatives of the species, *Homo sapiens*.'

'I don't know nothing about that jasper with the beard,' the cowhand stated, trying not to show he was close to being

[4] For the benefit of new readers: an explanation of the term, 'right bower', is given in *Footnote Six, APPENDIX TWO*. J.T.E.

overawed by the man's flow of eloquence. 'But I wouldn't go calling *Mark Counter* no "hommy sappy-yan", or whichever you-all say it. He's a good ole boy from Texas, like me, and he for sure wouldn't take kind to you thinking, or saying, he was some kind of foreigner.'

'I'll retain the matter in mind, should I make the acquaintance of Mr Counter,' the Bostonian promised jovially. 'But how remiss of us. We are delaying you from partaking of liquid refreshment in yonder festive hostelry, my good sir. Please accept my gratitude and felicitations for having been so kind as to satisfy our curiosity.'

'Shucks, I was right pleased to do it,' the Texan declared and, accepting there was no chance of extending the chance acquaintance, he nodded more to the woman than her companion, then strolled across the sidewalk trying to remember some of the man's long words with which to impress the other members of his trail crew.

'What was all that about, Ozzie?' the girl inquired, after the cowhand had disappeared into the saloon, her voice suggesting she had been raised in the same city as her companion although at a somewhat lower level of its society.

'I was in the process of envisaging how a man with such Herculean thews might prove of the most inestimable service to us in our current field of endeavour, my dear Charlotte,' the man replied, staring pensively at where the wagon had been when it was raised in such a spectacular fashion to have its wheel replaced. 'He could, in fact, solve our most pressing problem. To whit, the provision of the means by which we may gain ingress to the Wells Fargo office in the absence of the manager and all other employees of that most estimable company.'

'So *that's* it!' Charlotte Solikin ejaculated, but quietly, having grown accustomed to Oswald Nolly's bombastic way of speaking. Darting a quick glance about her to make sure they were not being overheard, she went on eagerly, 'And you'll want *me* to persuade him to help us?'

'Which *"him"* might that be, my dear?' the man queried, although he had a pretty good idea of the answer and noticed that the girl was contemplating the prospect favourably.

'That cowboy, of course,' Charlotte replied.

'That *cowboy*, as you so naïvely term him, is one of the very last people I would want to become cognisant with the facts of what we are here to do, my dear,' Nolly declared and, despite the expression of endearment, his voice held a grim warning. 'In fact, his name was prominent among those of whom I was cautioned to beware when embarking upon this venture. While he is no longer a member of the town's police department – or whatever the minions of law and order are called here in the hinterland – the same still applies. It was, unfortunately for your hopes, the other Herculean giant of whom I was thinking.'

'The *other*?' Charlotte repeated, her voice losing its enthusiasm, and she did not trouble to conceal her disappointment. 'Aw, Ossie, he's nothing but an over-sized, dull-witted hayseed.'

'As you say, my dear, as you say,' the Bostonian admitted. 'Yet those are the very qualities which make him the man we require.'

'Maybe,' the girl sniffed. 'But it won't be anywhere so much fun.'

'Possibly not, my dove, possibly no – !' Nolly conceded, almost sympathetically, reaching into his jacket's right side outer pocket. His commiseration ended abruptly and a startled expression came to his face as he spat out, 'What the – ?'

'What's wrong?' Charlotte demanded, startled by the vehemence with which her companion had uttered the last two words and watching as he began a hurried search of his other pockets.

'I – I've been *robbed*!' Nolly replied, in tones of incredulity, but he had regained sufficient composure to speak softly.

'*Robbed?*' the girl gasped, so surprised she showed less discretion and raised her voice a little. However, nobody took any notice of her apart from her companion. A look of delight came to her face and, although she had the presence of mind to moderate her tone, she went on, 'Just wait until the boys at the Boylston Street Lobster Kitchen hear that Ossie Nolly was "high dived" on the street of a hick town!'

'Most *amusing*!' the Bostonian growled, as he glared at the young woman with concentrated fury, being aware that to be 'high dived' was to have one's pocket picked.

'I'm sorry, Ossie!' Charlotte apologised, having no illusions about the portly man's nature when crossed or roused and losing her levity immediately. ' 'As he taken your wallet?'

'If only he *had*!' Nolly replied bitterly. 'He's lifted my *pocketbook* – And there is enough in it to permit anybody with a modicum of knowledge where such matters are concerned to ascertain exactly what we have in mind.'

'Are you sure you had it – ?' Charlotte began soothingly, hoping to reduce the wrath caused by her incautious reference to the reaction of their associates in Boston.

'Of course I *did*!' Nolly growled, showing no sign of being mollified. 'You don't *think* I'd leave it in my hotel room, where a maid might find and read it, do you?'

'No,' the girl admitted, deciding it would be unwise to comment on how ill-advised she had always considered her companion's habit of committing incriminating details of illicit activities to paper. 'It's just that I wouldn't have believed *anybody* was good enough to "pocket prowl" *you* and get away with it.'

'Egad, my dear, that such a thought should have eluded *me*!' the Bostonian answered, looking a trifle less furious. 'There is much merit in your assertion, I'll admit. Only a "fingersmith" of exceptional ability could have done so, even while I was engrossed in watching the rubes parading by and contemplating upon how the bearded giant might be of assistance. And the light of one so extremely capable is unlikely to be kept concealed beneath a bushel.'

'So you think Folbert will know him?' Charlotte guessed, referring to the owner of a small saloon in which the other members of the Bostonian's gang had taken accommodation while she and he were occupying rooms at the much more luxurious Railroad House Hotel.

'I would be inclined to answer your supposition in the affirmative, my dear,' Nolly declared. 'So hie yourself thence and obtain audience with him. If he is cognisant with the cognomen, or appellation of the miscreant, inform our associates so they may take the appropriate measures.'

'What do you want them to do?' the girl inquired, despite having formed an accurate assessment of the form the instructions would take.

'Regain possession of my property, of course,' Nolly replied, as had been anticipated by his companion. 'Ascertain whether the said miscreant has scrutinised the contents of the pocketbook and show him the wisdom of exercising greater discretion in the selection of his victims in the future. I trust carrying out the task will not be beyond the reach of their somewhat limited intellectual capabilities.'

'Aren't you coming with me?' Charlotte asked.

'No,' the Bostonian answered, in a manner which warned the girl any argument would be unwelcome. 'I shall remain here and subject that bearded and gigantic yokel to a closer scrutiny with the purpose of ascertaining whether he will prove of service to us.'

CHAPTER SIX

YELL AND I'LL KILL YOU!

'The name's Crumble, gents,' announced the man whose timely arrival had helped Mark Counter to make possible the removal of the wagon. 'I wouldn't want to tell you the name my momma saddled me with. So I may's well say's I've come to be called "Tiny", 'though I don't know how, or why.'

'Now me,' drawled the Ysabel Kid, the blond giant having taken the opportunity to perform introductions after he and the bearded stranger had accepted the free drinks offered by the owner of Henry's Saloon. They had also received further congratulations over their feat of strength from all sides. 'I don't know what else you-all could've expected folks to call you.'

'Which's just about what you'd expect from somebody who has a damned great *white* stallion and calls it *"Nigger"*,' Frank Derringer claimed, shaking hands with the big man. He found, as the black dressed Texan had, the grip he received was firm, yet gentle, and went on, 'Right pleased to make your acquaintance, Tiny. Only I wish you pair had let me know you could hoist up the wagon. That way, I could've bet Lon a couple of dollars you'd do it.'

'You'll all notice's he was only game to put a bet down happen he was certain sure of winning?' the Kid scoffed. 'There's some's'd allow you'd be doing no more'n your right and legal duty by the good tax paying citizens of this here fair city was you-all to run such tinhorns out of it.'

'Likely,' Marshal Kail Beauregard replied, the latter part of the comment having been directed to him. Then he shook hands with Tiny, continuing, 'Anyways, thanks once again for helping out, Tiny.'

'Shucks, it warn't nothing, Marshal,' the big man answered. 'Like I said, I'm allus happy to lend a hand with any lifting 'n' toting's comes along.'

'Talking of which, Frank,' Beauregard said, swinging his gaze to the gambler. 'What was you-all saying to Mr Walton while all the lifting and toting was going on?'

'Just passing the time of day, sociable-like,' Derringer lied blandly. 'I thought he might need a reminder about how dangerous it could be for Mark and Tiny was he to forget to keep the horses standing still.'

'Did you figure he had it in mind to let them start walking, accidental-like of course, before the wheel was back on?' the marshal asked.

'Well now, I wouldn't want to go so far as to say he *told* me he'd something like that in mind,' Derringer confessed. 'Any more than I'd want to come right out and say that's what I reckoned he was figuring on doing, seeing as how he *didn't* do it.'

'Now if that's not just like a sneaky tinhorn!' the Kid snorted. 'He wouldn't say a plain ole "yes" was you to find him hanging and ask happen he wanted you to cut him down.'

'Was it you offering to help, I'd want to look down and make sure there wasn't something sharp or bad to be dropped on after you'd cut,' Derringer countered. 'Anyways, I noticed that you suddenly got to be conspicuous by your absence when there was some lifting needed. Which wasn't any great surprise, I suppose. Any time a blasted Comanche figures there might be some work needs doing, he calls up his squaws to do it.'

'What in hell else're women for?' the Kid inquired, having no objection to what some people might have considered a derogatory comment regarding his Indian blood as it was made by a good and loyal friend.

'He means *that*, you know,' the gambler informed the rest of the party soberly. 'I keep thinking it's high time either you or Dusty told him about the birds, the bees and the flowers, Mark.'

'We've thought on it some, but concluded it wasn't any too smart a notion,' the blond giant replied. 'Happen we did, he might start in to raising a whole bunch of young'n's just like him and damned if *one's* not more than enough.'

'I do so know about the birds, the bees and the flowers, blast it!' the Kid protested in what appeared to be genuine indignation. 'But it's just a *loco* white-eyes' notion and don't work worth a hoot. Why, I got me a bird, a bee and a flower one time 'n' put 'em all together in a box.'

'What happened?' Beauregard asked.

'The bird ate the bee,' the Kid explained with a straight face, 'got diarrhoea, shit on the flower and killed it.'

'He did it, too,' Derringer insisted, when the laughter had died away. 'Thing being, Lon, which unfortunate female was you inflicting yourself on while the rest of us was working around the wagon?'

'I'm not allus a-chasing the gals like some jasper called Mark Counter's'll be left nameless,' the Kid objected, adopting an air of spurious conscious virtue, then turned his gaze to the bearded man. 'Do you allus leave your thirty-year gatherings tossed down in an alley, Tiny?'

'Huh?' the black haired giant grunted, then followed the direction in which the Indian dark Texan was glancing. 'This old pack of mine?'

'Nothing else but,' the Kid confirmed.

'Shucks,' Tiny replied. 'All it's got in it's a mess of furs 'n' hides I've fetched here to sell.'

'Which there's some's'd say's a pretty fair reason for not leaving it behind,' the Kid pointed out, the object in question and the Sharps Old Reliable rifle having been carried into the saloon by their owner.

'Maybe so,' Tiny conceded. 'But I only set it down 'cause I didn't reckon I'd be able to help Mark lift that itty bitty ole wagon with it on my back.'

'Well now, I don't reckon's you could've, comes to that,' the Kid admitted in a mock judicial fashion. 'Only there's safer places you-all could've left it. Like where you could've kept a watch on it, in case somebody took the notion to head off with it like it was their own.'

'Shucks,' the big man protested mildly, unaware that his words were being listened to with considerable interest by somebody other than the group with whom he was drinking beer. 'I didn't reckon, seeing what I was doing, anybody'd be ornery enough to touch it.'

Having sent Charlotte Solikin to deliver his instructions to their associates, Oswald Nolly had entered Henry's Saloon to conduct his examination of the man he hoped might offer the solution to his problem. Contriving to reach the counter sufficiently close to be able to eavesdrop on the conversation, he found the naïve comment he had just overheard most satisfying. It implied that the bearded giant might be so simple he could be tricked into doing what was required of him.

'Even with that being the case,' the Kid drawled, deciding Tiny was serious, 'there's still some's might've reckoned you should ought to have left it a mite closer to hand.'

'I didn't want it cluttering up the sidewalk,' the big man pointed out.

'Better that than lose it,' the Kid countered.

'Are you saying somebody tried to wideloop it, Lon?' Beauregard asked.

'Nope,' the Kid replied. 'I'm not *saying* that.'

'But somebody did *try*?' the marshal hinted, drawing the correct conclusion in spite of the way in which the answer had been phrased.

'Somebody *could've* been figuring on *trying*,' the black dressed Texan admitted. 'Only he telled me's how he was only going to cut it open so's he could see if the feller's owned it'd left a name and address inside, him concluding it'd been lost unnoticed and accidental-like.'

'And you *believed* him?' Derringer suggested.

'Just about's much's I allus believe *you-all*,' the Kid asserted, 'Which, should you tell me's how Monday comes the day before Tuesday, I'd just natural' take a look at the calendar to see was that right.'

'So where-all's this helpful jasper at, Lon?' the marshal asked.

'I don't know to the inch of ground he's on right now,' the Kid confessed. 'He got away and took off running.'

'Why didn't you go after him and fetch him back?' the gambler challenged.

'On *foot*?' the Kid yelped, registering extreme horror at the suggestion.

'They're not put at the bottom of your legs just to stop your ankle-bones bumping on the ground when you get down off your horse,' Derringer pointed out. 'You can *walk*, or even *run* on them once in a while.'

'So I've been told, only I've heard it's even worse'n taking baths for weakening a man,' the Kid answered, then gave a shrug. 'Anyways, didn't seem to me like there was no call to go wasting sweat 'n' boot leather over him, seeing's how he hadn't gotten into the pack to take nothing.'

'Who is he, Lon?' Beauregard inquired, feeling certain that such a lenient attitude would only have been adopted if the man was known to the black dressed young Texan and could be located should the need arise.

'Calls his-self "Reg Wall",' the Kid replied, confirming the peace officer's supposition. 'Which, was I asked's likely only a "summer name".'[1]

'Dusty told me that you'd had word he'd come to town,' the marshal stated. 'But I thought his game's picking pockets.'

'Mine's supposed to be *riding* scout, but way things've been going just recent', I've had to go *walking* the rounds as a deputy,' the Kid countered. 'Anyways, it was him for sure. I'd had him pointed out to me down to Folbert's night after he hit town.'

'He's not done anything's we've heard tell of since he came in,' Mark supplemented. 'Which's why Dusty hasn't sent a couple of us 'round to pick up his toes.'

'I reckon you-all must've scared him off afore he could start dipping into folk's pockets out front of the saloon,' the Kid guessed. 'He allowed he hadn't, which he'd've done whether he had or not likely. Only I don't reckon he'd've took a chance on trying to cut into Tiny's pack if he'd been lucky in his wide-looping from the crowd.'

'It could be,' Beauregard admitted. 'At least, if he did rob anybody before he got to the pack, none of them have found out about it yet. You-all know where I can find him, should I have need to?'

'He's bunked down at Ma Pinker's rooming house,' the Kid answered, the marshal's final sentence having been more of a statement than a question. 'For a spell, anyways. Likely I shouldn't've done, but I sort of hinted he'd be a whole heap

[1] 'Summer name' : an alias. J.T.E.

happier in some other town. What was said, he's figuring on taking the evening train out.'

'I'll drift by Ma Pinker's and say, "*Adios, amigo*," to him as soon as I've looked in at the office and asked if there's anything else needs 'tending to,' Beauregard declared, deducing correctly why the Kid had allowed Wall to depart and setting his seal of approval on the way the matter had been handled. Emptying the schooner of beer he was holding, behaving in the casually determined manner of a competent peace officer who was on the point of resuming his duties, he departed after saying, 'I'll likely be seeing you-all down to the Fair Lady later in the day.'

A growing sensation of foreboding had assailed Oswald Nolly as he eavesdropped upon the conversation. Nor was his perturbation lessened as he contemplated the implications of the line of action proposed by the marshal.

On hearing the references to Wall's criminal proclivities and presence in the vicinity at the time he was being robbed, the Bostonian had temporarily put aside his interest in Tiny Crumble. The information he had acquired was both useful and very disturbing. While he had learned an address at which the pickpocket might be located – and this would help should Folbert be unable to supply such a detail – he had also been made aware of how imperative it was for his men to find Wall as quickly as possible. The scheme upon which they were engaged would be ruined if the 'fingersmith' was to fall into the hands of such an obviously efficient peace officer while still in possession of the stolen property. Furthermore, even after the pocketbook had been retrieved, it would be most inadvisable to allow Wall to be taken into custody. If he had read the contents, he was likely to make use of what he had discovered in an attempt to bargain for his freedom.

Watching the marshal walking away, Nolly finished in a gulp the drink at which he had been sipping while listening. Then he turned and left the saloon with the intention of doing all he could to ensure that the threat to his scheme was removed.

* * * * *

Unaware that his only successful theft so far that day had placed his life in danger, Reg Wall was leaning against the end of a building on a deserted street. To all outward appearances, he was merely sheltering the flame of a match while lighting a cigarette. He was, however, listening to the footsteps of an intended victim approaching through the alley behind him.

Despite his pressing need for money – having taken the conversation he had had with the Ysabel Kid very much to heart – Wall had decided against rejoining the festive crowds to acquire it by his favourite means. Although there had been no direct mention of it, he had concluded the Texan was aware that picking pockets was his speciality and he felt sure the marshal shared the knowledge. So he would be the first suspect if any thefts of that nature were reported. However, while he realised this would be the case when his sole victim discovered the loss of the pocketbook and handkerchief, he had been disinclined to throw them away until he procured some other loot.

Having put distance between himself and the Kid, Wall had been on the point of looking into the pocketbook to ascertain whether it held money, which could not be identified, before discarding it. Before he could do so, he had seen what might offer an opportunity to improve his dire financial straits in a manner which would make him a less obvious suspect when the victim complained to the marshal. Certainly the means he was now contemplating lacked any of the subtlety and skill required when he was picking pockets.

On discovering that he appeared to have to himself the back street in the business area, Wall had been trying to select the most suitable target for a burglary when he had noticed a woman entering the other end of the alley he was passing. Sombrely dressed, bespectacled, somewhat bulky in build and determined looking rather than attractive, he would have ignored her if he had been in more affluent circumstances. However, despite her apparently formidable demeanour, his present impoverished condition led him to consider her as a potential prey. The direction from which she was coming, her attire, the way she was burdened with an umbrella, reticule and carpetbag had all combined to suggest she had arrived on the west-bound train. So he had concluded that robbing her could prove profitable. At the worst, even if there was nothing of value in the carpetbag, he hoped to find money in the reticule.

The problem with which Wall had been confronted was how to gain possession of the woman's property and avoid falling foul of the law when he had done so. Lacking the cover offered by a crowd, he could not hope to 'high dive' her reticule without being detected. Nor would snatching it from her hand and running away serve his purpose any better. She was sure to start screaming for help and, despite the apparent deserted nature of the street, somebody might overhear and come to investigate. Even if no assistance was forthcoming, she would be able to reach the marshal and, in all probability, offer a description of him far too quickly for safety.

Having decided that he could not employ two methods which had produced satisfactory results in the past had done nothing to lessen Wall's resolve to carry out the robbery. Provided it could be performed without entailing any risk to himself, he had never hesitated to use violence.

Nearer came the sound of footsteps!

To the pickpocket's satisfaction, the woman turned away instead of towards him. What was more, implying that his presence had not aroused suspicion, she continued to walk at the same pace.

Discarding the cigarette and match as having served their purpose, Wall swung around. Taking a quick glance in each direction to satisfy himself there was nobody else in sight, he darted after the woman. Before she could respond to his approach in any way, he threw his right arm over her shoulder until it was pressing against her throat and his left hand grasped the back of her jacket's collar.

'Yell and I'll kill you!' the pickpocket warned as he tightened his two holds, employing a vicious snarl which he also tried to make sound like the drawl of a Texan.

Although the woman's body stiffened, she made no attempt to resist as her assailant swung her around. Nor, despite dropping the umbrella, reticule and carpetbag, did she offer to struggle while being forced to return into the alley. However, for all her submissive behaviour, Wall began to appreciate that his control of the situation was far from being a sinecure. They were almost the same height, there being only about an inch and a couple of pounds' weight in his favour. His right arm might be in a position to keep her quiet, but only so long as he had it held across her windpipe. Unfortunately, he must take it away before he could go through the contents of the reticule and carpetbag. Unless he could terrify her sufficiently to ensure she remain silent, there was a danger that she would start to scream as soon as he presented her with an opportunity. Being aware of how Westerners regarded a man who molested a member of the weaker sex, he had no desire to incur the penalty should the commotion bring somebody to find out what was causing it.

Thinking fast while compelling his captive to go in the required direction, the pickpocket came up with what he considered to be the best solution to his dilemma. He would fling her, face first and with all the force he could muster, against the wall of the nearer building. Then, if the impact did not render her insensible, she would be too winded to raise an outcry before he could draw his revolver and use its butt to ensure her silence. Given good luck, she would at most be able to offer only a vague description of her assailant when she regained consciousness. Possibly, should she remember the way he had spoken and should she possess the kind of antipathy which many Kansans felt for the visitors from the Lone Star State, she would claim her attacker was a Texan. In which case, it would still further reduce the chance of the marshal considering him as a possible suspect for the assault.

Even as Wall was drawing his conclusions, but before he could put them into effect, things began to go wrong!

Pausing to gather his strength for the thrust he intended to give his captive, the pickpocket felt her going limp and she slumped a little until she was leaning against him. Caught unawares by the unexpected pressure of her weight, he was thrown off balance and inadvertently relaxed his grips slightly. His belief that terror had caused her to faint was rapidly disillusioned.

Changing from apparently passive compliance to rapid and purposeful motion, the woman brought up her right hand to catch hold of his right bicep in a surprisingly firm grip. Exhibiting an equal strength, her left fingers and thumb enfolded his right wrist. While this was happening, working with the smooth co-ordination indicative of considerable practise, she thrust her right leg to the rear until its knee was touching the ground, and bent the left. By hauling down and to the left on the trapped arm, she completed the destruction of her assailant's equilibrium.

A howl of alarm burst from Wall as he felt his feet leaving the ground. Turning a half somersault, the contents cascaded from his jacket's pockets and the revolver fell out of its holster. For all that, he might have counted himself fortunate. Such was the speed of the unexpected attack, it happened too quickly for his mind to appreciate what was happening and he could not counter the throw. So, although he alighted supine and partially winded in front of his intended victim, the result was less severe than if he had tried to resist.

Thrusting herself erect and releasing her holds as the would-be attacker landed, the woman did not behave as might have been expected under the circumstances. Instead of starting to shout for help, or hurrying away, she stepped around and, coming to a halt with feet spread apart and arms akimbo, gazed down at the pickpocket.

'Trying to make me think you're a Texan, for shame,' the intended victim chided and her voice, while mockingly grim, sounded far younger than when she had been speaking with Waco in the waiting room at the railroad depot. 'You-all didn't sound even a little bit like one and no Southerner gentleman would have aimed to throw a lady face-first against a wall, then whomp her over the head with a gun butt.'

Startled by the discovery that his attempted deception had failed and his intentions been discerned, Wall sucked air into his lungs while forcing himself slowly into a sitting position.

Under different conditions, the pickpocket might have been puzzled by the surprising behaviour of the woman. At that moment, however, he did not give it a moment's thought. Instead, his sole consideration was directed to finding a way to escape from his predicament. He felt sure that, in spite of the way she was acting, his intended victim would not allow the matter to rest and meant to have him arrested. Shaking his head to clear it, his gaze went to where the Navy

Colt lay near the loot from the earlier and more successful robbery.

Sucking in a breath, Wall suddenly made a grab for the weapon!

Once again, the woman proved fully capable of protecting herself. Hitching her skirt to above the level of her knees, she displayed a pair of calf high brown boots as suitable for riding a horse as walking and black silk stockings, all of which were far more stylish than her outer garments. Stepping forward swiftly, she swung her right foot in a power packed kick. The toe of her boot caught Wall under the chin, snapping his head to the rear and causing him to pitch over helplessly, the revolver flying from his hand. As the back of his skull struck the ground, bright lights erupted briefly before his eyes and then everything went black.

Letting out a snort of disdain, the woman was about to walk away when she noticed the pocketbook lying alongside her unconscious would-be assailant. Concluding that such an expensive item was unlikely to be his property and in all probability had been stolen rather than merely found after being dropped by accident, she decided to teach him a further lesson. Picking up the book, she opened it with the intention of seeing if there was anything inside to identify its owner. Although it contained no name, she found the contents very interesting.

'Hm!' the woman said pensively, having read the details of Oswald Nolly's scheme, looking down at the still motionless pickpocket. 'I don't reckon a knobhead like you could have the brains to come up with something like *this*. And I can't think how you came to get hold of the book, but I wouldn't want to be in *your* shoes should its owner lay hands on you. Anyway, it's none of *my* business and I don't intend to get involved.'

Closing the book while delivering the final sentiment, the woman returned it to Wall's pocket and tucked the handkerchief in after it. Leaving the alley, she glanced around to make sure the incident had gone unobserved. Assured it had and she could depart without being called up to answer awkward questions, she retrieved her property and walked swiftly off in the direction she had been going before the attempt was made to rob her.

As with the woman's response to the shooting she had witnessed outside the railroad depot, the way she was behaving indicated she must be something other than was suggested by her appearance. To any chance onlooker, it would have seemed she regarded as an everyday occurrence having to defend herself from bodily harm and saw nothing out of the ordinary in reading the plans for a robbery which, providing one problem could be solved, was being contemplated.

CHAPTER SEVEN

I WOULDN'T WANT HIM RILED AT *ME*

'Who-all'd be a lawman?' the Ysabel Kid inquired, with blatantly spurious sympathy, after having watched Marshal Kail Beauregard go through the front door of Henry's Saloon. Knowing nothing of the reason for it, he had noticed, without paying any attention, Oswald Nolly's departure almost on the heels of the peace officer. 'They're allus having to go chasing off some place or another, while us good law abiding and tax paying citizens can stand back and take things easy.'

'Just how do *you* get to be one of *us* good law abiding and tax paying citizens, you blasted border smuggler?' Frank Derringer challenged and, finishing his schooner of beer, continued. 'Have you *ever* known him to be good for *anything*, Mark, much less law abiding and tax paying.'

'I've never known him to be *anything* paying, truth to tell,' the blond giant declared, also emptying his glass and, placing it on the counter, looking pointedly from it to his black dressed companion. 'Especially when it comes to buying smokes – or drinks.'

'I should reckon not, for shame!' the Kid protested, exuding what appeared to be an air of self righteous virtue. 'If it wasn't for *us*, you blasted white folks wouldn't have got the tobacco to smoke in the first place and it's again' the legal law to sell, or let a good ole Injun boy like me buy drinking liquor.'

'This varmint can come up with more sneaky ways to avoid parting with his money than any *six* people I know,' the gambler informed Tiny Crumble.

'I dunno,' Mark Counter objected. 'Waco runs him a close second.'

'That's for sure,' Derringer conceded. 'There's one modest

young cuss, if I ever saw one. Why you can stand alongside him in a bar all night and you'd never know he'd got a thin dime in his pocket.'

'He likely wouldn't have, happen he'd been fool enough to play cards with you-all,' the Kid declared. 'And I don't reckon it's right for you to go telling Tiny the boy's cheap when he's not here to prove he *is*. Anyways, you know his trouble's that he's got right short arms and keeps his money awful deep in his pockets.'

'You won't get any arguments from me about *that*,' Derringer asserted, then looked at the slimmer of the Texans with well simulated truculence and disdain. 'Which, next time I run across Clay Allison, I'm going to ask him whether the boy was always so inclined, or if he only got took that way *after* he'd had the misfortune to fall in with evil companions.'

'He for certain sure fell in with one when he met up with you-all and got led from the straight 'n' narrow path,' the Kid countered. 'Leastwise, it wasn't *me's* taught him how to cheat at cards and all them sneaky ways of tricking folks out of their money.'

'I don't bring to mind *ever* seeing *you* play cards and don't reckon you'd even know *how*,' Derringer answered, instead of explaining that he had given the youngster instruction in cheating methods and included details of how various confidence tricks were worked with the best of intentions. 'Fact being, I'll bet just about the only game *you* could teach him to cheat at would be that "hands" you blasted Comanche play instead of something civilised like poker.'

'And he'd be the one to do it, what I've been told,' Mark commented to the bearded giant, as soberly as if imparting information of the greatest importance rather than participating in the kind of banter which did much to cement the strong bonds linking himself and his companions. 'According to his lodge brothers, who should *know*, he even cheats when he's playing *nanip-ka*.'[1]

'Damned if these varmints aren't ganging up on lil ole me

[1] For the benefit of new readers: explanations of how to play the Indian gambling game, 'hands' and *nanip'ka*, 'guess over the hill' – a method by which children were taught to locate hidden enemies – are given in: *COMANCHE*. J.T.E.

again!' the Kid wailed. 'I wish the boy was here to help me share some of the load.'

'Knowing him, he'd be more likely to add to it,' Derringer claimed. 'Anyways, he should be here soon. He only went along to the railroad depot to see if the present that he's sent off for to give Babsy has arrived.'

'Happen it has, we'll not be seeing him for a spell yet,' Mark announced. 'Seeing he knows how Freddie and Dusty'll be busy dealing with all those high mucky-mucks who've come for the parade, he'll likely have taken it straight to the Fair Lady and'll be using it as an excuse to find out whether Babsy's got more hair on her chest than he has on his.'

'At *this* time of the day?' the gambler asked.

'Leave us not forget's he's been spending a heap of time in right bad company,' the Kid pointed out and the direction in which he was gazing signified clearly that it was the blond giant to whom he was referring. 'So he's certain sure to have picked up such bad habits along the trail.'

'That could be so,' Derringer admitted. 'And, happen you've called it right, we'll not be seeing him for a spell.'

'I wouldn't want to count on it,' Mark stated, without offering to refute his companions' imputations. 'Fact being, knowing him, he's likely delivered the present and's waiting outside until *somebody* gets 'round to setting up the drinks.'

'Here!' Tiny said, hurriedly dipping his right hand into his trousers' hip pocket and bringing out a far from bulky purse. 'I'll get them.'

'Hell, *amigo*,' the blond giant ejaculated, having been on the point of ordering another round. 'There's no call for *you* to do that.'

'I'll "angle" along with Mark that there's not, happen it isn't against the house rules,'[2] Derringer went on, also appreciating how the trend of the conversation could have been misinterpreted by the bearded giant. Having only recently made their acquaintance, he could not be expected to know

[2] 'Angle' : a gambling term meaning to enter into a private arrangement with another player – i.e. to split the pot evenly regardless of which participant wins it, or to refrain from raising against one another unless doing so would be advantageous in forcing out the other players – and prohibited in many games. J.T.E.

that accusing the Kid of being reluctant to buy drinks or tobacco was an accepted, if untruthful, practice with them. 'What we're *trying* to do is shame this baby-faced cuss into setting up a round of drinks for the first time in his young and sin-filled life.'

'Shucks, I've not had what could be called a whole heap of doings with the Comanch', seeing's I've never met any of 'em, but I've come to know a mite about Injuns and'd sort of figured *that* all along the trail,' Tiny answered, extracting a twenty dollar gold piece from the purse and, watching with some anxiety how his words were being received, ready to halt them if necessary. 'So, happen the *Tshaoh*[3] think like the kind I've had dealings with, Lon's likely helping his kin to save enough to buy back Manhattan Island for the same price that Dutch jasper gave for it.[4] Which being, I don't reckon's how it'd be the right'n' Christian thing to make him go squandering any of his *easy* earned money buying drinks for us fellers.'

'Well I'll be 'ternally damned to the fiery furnaces,' the Kid groaned, turning his gaze upwards as if in search of support from the heavens. 'Which, afore I get told from all sides, ain't *nobody*, 'cepting me doubts. He's not been with this shiftless pair of varmints half an hour yet and they've already got him to siding with 'em in abusing poor lil ole me. So all right, I'll set up the son-of-a-bitching drinks same's I *allus* wind up doing.'

'Aw no, Lon,' Tiny protested, delighted by the black dressed Texan's comment and the sight of the broad grin which had come to the faces of Mark and Derringer while he was making his reply. Such reactions indicated no offence had been taken by any of them over his reference to the Kid's Indian blood. 'I'd feel a heap better if you'd let *me* get them 'stead of you.'

'Well, so be it then,' the Kid replied, giving what could have been a shrug of reluctant resignation. 'Seeing's how your

[3] For the benefit of new readers: an explanation of the word, '*Tshaoh*', is given in: Footnote 2, *APPENDIX THREE.* J.T.E.

[4] The purchase of Manhattan Island was made by Peter Minuit, Director General of what was at that time the Dutch colony of New Netherlands, the price paid being, 'pieces of bright cloth, beads and other trinkets to the value of sixty guilders', or about twenty-four dollars. J.T.E.

health's at stake, I'll just have to haul back on the reins and let you.'

'Why thank you' most to death for being so kind and considerate to a poor, passing stranger,' Tiny countered and signalled to a bartender who was approaching. 'Would you kindly draw four more beers, friend?'

'Is this your first time in Mulrooney, *amigo*?' Mark inquired, after the order had been delivered and paid for, watching the bearded giant accept a handful of change and put it into the purse without checking whether the amount he received was correct.

'It surely is,' Tiny confirmed, pocketing the purse and waving his other hand to the bulky pack. 'Just recently I've sort of been taking the notion that maybe those feller's come out to the back country to buy hides and furs from us hunting folk are paying a whole heap less than they're worth for 'em. So I reckoned, seeing how *everybody* allows Mulrooney's a honest and fair dealing town, I'd drop by and see what kind of price I can get here.'

'You shouldn't have any difficulty finding somebody to take them off your hands,' Mark declared, pleased by the compliment to the town as he and his companions had helped give it the good reputation. 'Fact being, should you want, we could introduce you to a feller who will. But, seeing what day it is, you'll have to wait until tomorrow morning to get him in a mood to dicker.'

'I'd admire to meet him and don't mind waiting,' Tiny answered, appreciating how beneficial the introduction would be, but thinking ruefully of how little money he had with him. 'Fact being, I sort of took the notion I'd likely have to's soon's I got off the stage. Dog-my-cats if I hadn't clean forgotten Independence Day was coming up until I saw the decorations.'

'It does tend to sneak up on you,' Derringer said and raised his schooner of beer. 'Here's to a good sale for your furs.'

'Hey though,' Tiny drawled, when the Texans had echoed the gambler's good wishes. 'I don't reckon's how, being in a place this fancy, a feller can just open up the front of his pants and cut loose like he was out in the piney woods. So where's he go happen he's got to go and do it?'

'Through the door at the end of the bar, along the passage

and out back,' Mark supplied. 'There's a four-holer to the left.'

'I've never figured out why Henry don't blaze a trail to it,' the Kid asserted. Then, indicating the blond giant and Derringer with a derisory wave of his left hand, he went on, 'At least this pair haven't got 'round to teaching you all of their sneaky ways yet. 'Cause, happen they had've, you'd've knowed to ask where the backhouse was and gone afore *they* got a chance to slicker you into buying for 'em. Which's why they *didn't* teach you that one, was you-all to ask.'

'Well I'll swan!' Tiny ejaculated, in a voice filled with mock admiration. 'A man learn's something new 'n' useless every minute he's around you, Lon.'

'Was you three foot shorter 'n' two hundred pounds lighter, I'd get riled over that,' the Kid threatened. 'But, seeing's you aren't I'll let you off easy and do nothing at all.'

'Which's what you do best,' Mark declared. 'We'll watch he doesn't wide-loop your beer while you're gone, Tiny.'

'Now there's a right friendly and likeable feller,' Derringer appraised, as the bearded giant went through the door which allowed customers to reach the toilets outside the saloon. 'And he's a whole lot smarter and better educated than he strikes you at first sight.'

'Trouble being,' the Kid said soberly. 'Going by the way he left his pack in the alley when he came to help Mark and just now pocketed his change without counting it, I'd say he's a mite too trustful for his own good.'

'It's be a sorry old world if *everybody* was as mean and distrustful as *you*,' the gambler declared, despite agreeing with the Indian-dark Texan's sentiments. 'Henry makes sure his bartenders don't short change the customers, so there's no need to check what your given in here.'

'I'm not gainsaying that,' the Kid asserted. 'And he'd be just's safe in most of the other places around town, but not all of them. Which, seeing as how it was Freddie and us who got Mulrooney the kind of rep' for square dealing's brought him here, I reckon it's our bounden duty to sort of keep an eye on him and make sure nothing happens to get him figuring he's heard wrong.'

'I had something along those lines in mind myself,' Mark

admitted, although he felt sure his motives differed from those of his black dressed *amigo*.

'It wouldn't do to let him take the notion we figure he needs wet-nursing, though,' Derringer warned, drawing a wrong conclusion where Mark's comment was concerned. 'Because, happen he should, I'm going to make good and sure he knows whose fool idea it was, *Lon*. Strong as he is, I wouldn't want him riled up at me.'

'I'm not thinking he needs wet-nursing as such,' Mark corrected. 'But, like you said, Frank, the gentle way he talks and acts could give somebody wrong notions about him.'

' 'Less I'm mistaken,' the Kid stated. 'Which it's not often I am, but anybody who does get wrong notions about him could right sudden get 'round to wishing they hadn't.'

'That's what I mean, Lon,' the blond giant replied, having guessed instinctively at a problem which was frequently faced by the other exceptionally big man and knowing it would not have occurred to his smaller companions. 'Good natured as he is, I still don't reckon Tiny would take kindly to having some smart-assed son-of-a-bitch treating him like he was stupid. Trouble is, when you've got Tiny's size and strength, you can all too easily hurt somebody real bad without meaning to should you get pushed into losing your temper. Once you've done it, folks don't sit back and think of what made you do it, only that you've busted up somebody smaller than you. Which's why I reckon we should try to get him to stay around us. There'll be less chance of it happening if he does.'

'You've got a good point there,' Derringer remarked, realising he had never heard the big blond speak with such feeling. 'And, even if you hadn't, I've took a liking to Tiny and reckon it'd be right neighbourly to let him know he's among friends.'

'Saying *you* like him's no way of doing *that*,' the Kid claimed, also having been impressed by the way Mark had spoken. 'Hey though, something else's just come to mind. Seeing's how he's come in on the stage, he'll not have had time yet to look around for a place to bed down and, way folks've been coming in from every which way for the celebrating, he'll be hard put to find anywhere.'

'That's another reason for having him stay around us,' the blond giant asserted. 'He didn't look to have much money in his poke and prices hereabout likely come higher than he's used to, or had counted on. The kind of place he could afford would be the kind where he'd most likely have somebody rile him up by taking him for a fool on account of how he looks and acts.'

Coming from a family in which exceptional size and muscular development were hereditary,[5] Mark had been taught at an early age just how dangerous the possession of such great strength could be if it was allowed to get out of control.[6] However, his physical appearance and general demeanour made him less susceptible than he suspected the bearded giant was to misapprehensions where his intelligence was concerned. As he was able to envisage and sympathise with the other's problem, he wanted to help Tiny to avoid being subjected to the kind of provocation which might lead to a loss of temper and an outburst of violence that could bring him into conflict with the law.

'Freddie will find him a room at the Fair Lady if he'll go there with us and'll be willing to hold the price down to what he can afford,' the Kid stated. 'And, even if he's already got some place in mind, I reckon he'll be willing to come along. What he said, he's not likely to know anybody in town apart from us. So he'll likely be pleased to have the company.'

'*Some* of it, anyways,' Derringer conceded, his pointed glance at the slimmer Texan showing where he felt reservations on the subject.

'Aw come on now, Frank,' the Kid objected. '*You're* not all that bad, nor the boy neither.'

'I wasn't meaning *me*,' Derringer explained, in mock patient tones. 'Or Waco, comes to the point. Although if *he* isn't all that bad, he'll surely do until somebody comes along who is.'

'Well now,' the Kid replied, looking as innocent as a choirboy about to receive a good conduct prize from the bishop.

[5] For the benefit of new readers: information regarding two of Mark Counter's descendants who inherited the family's muscular development is given in: Footnote Nine, *APPENDIX TWO*. J.T.E.

[6] A description of what happened on the occasion when, aroused by the sight of a man about to shoot at Waco – who was already lying seriously wounded – Mark Counter failed to hold his temper in check is given in: *Chapter Sixteen, 'A Little Knowledge'*, *RETURN TO BACKSIGHT*. J.T.E.

'Seeing's how it's not one or the other of you-all, what with Dusty being the boss 'n' Mark's bigger'n me, I for sure can't figure just who you could have in mind.'

'Then I'm not about to spoil your day by telling you,' Derringer declared. 'Thing being though, just in case it should be taken wrong, which of you *two* is figuring on doing the inviting?'

'Why's it got to be one of *us* two?' the Kid challenged. 'You're supposed to be the gambling man.'

'I'm a *professional* gambling man,' Derringer pointed out. 'Which means I've learned good enough sense to let other folks take the fool chances.'

'Hey, Mark!' one of the bartenders called, coming hurriedly out of the liquor store behind the counter, before any more could be said. 'That big feller's helped you lift the wagon's got his-self into a fight with some gandy dancers.'[7]

[7] 'Gandy dancer'; colloquialism for a railroad construction worker. J.T.E.

CHAPTER EIGHT

HE JUMPED US FOR NO REASON

Considering his financial position caused Tiny Crumble to lose some of his cheerful frame of mind as he walked along the passage between the liquor store and the room in which, although he was unaware of the fact, private high stake poker games were held, towards the rear entrance of Henry's Saloon. He had taken a liking to Mark Counter, the Ysabel Kid and Frank Derringer and believed it to be mutual. In his opinion, men of their kind would not have passed such derogatory remarks about one another – or the absent 'boy', Waco – even in jest while in the presence of a stranger unless they had accepted him as an equal and a friend. Nor would they have approved of the reference to the Kid being part Comanche if it had come from somebody they regarded in an unfavourable light.

The realisation that he had gained the trio's approbation caused the big man to feel more relaxed and at ease than he had since leaving the stagecoach on his arrival. Despite all he had heard about the fair and honest way in which Mulrooney was run, remembering unpleasant incidents in smaller towns he had visited, he had had misgivings about making the journey.

Mark had been correct in his analysis of the problems created by the bearded giant's physical appearance and demeanour.

Ever since Tiny could remember, having always been much larger than the average for his age, his size and bulk had set him apart from others of his generation. In spite of having been given a reasonable education, and possessing a gentle nature and a willingness to offer his services any time muscle power beyond the ordinary was required, he had found – with only rare exceptions such as the two Texans and the gambler – that people tended to regard him as something of a freak. Furthermore, as a result of his having learned while still a child that it was inadvisable for one of his build to dash about like his smaller companions and that he needed to take care in all his movements if he was not to inadvertently cause damage, his apparently slothful behaviour led many of those with whom he had come into contact to treat him with a pitying condescension which he had found most galling and hard to take.

There had been no suggestion of such an attitude on the part of any of the trio. However, although he was delighted at having received the suggestion that he should remain in their company and receive help in selling his furs, Tiny felt qualms over accepting the offer. Due to his failure to take into consideration that he would arrive on a public holiday, when there would be no business of that nature done, he might not have sufficient money to pay his way.

'Why you stubborn, evil hearted devil!' a harsh masculine voice bellowed, as the bearded giant was opening the back door. The speaker's accent was Irish and the words were sufficiently slurred to suggest he had taken several drinks. 'It's a lesson in manners I'll be after giving you!'

Stepping outside, Tiny saw something which drove away all thoughts of his dilemma.

The words were originating from a tallish, thickset, burly middle aged man wearing a well cut brown three piece suit, a white shirt, its collar and a multi-hued necktie sticking from the left side pocket of his jacket, and Hersome gaiter boots. Bareheaded, his red hair was close cropped and he had clean shaven, but flushed, rugged features. In his right hand, he grasped a heavy blackthorn walking stick and was clinging with the left to the reins of a snorting, wildly plunging burro which was clearly the object of his furious comment. Dirt smeared the back of his coat and the seat of his trousers and a new looking brown derby hat was lying on the ground close to his feet, suggesting that his anger was caused by having either fallen or been thrown off while he was attempting to ride the animal.

At the conclusion of the wrathful speech, the man launched a savage blow at the burro. Showing an appreciation of the danger, it jerked its head and backed hurriedly away. Taken unawares by the vigorous evasion, the tug on the reins he held not only caused the would-be assailant's stick to miss, but he found himself being dragged after the animal. Before he could stop himself, he had stepped upon and crushed the rounded crown of his curly brimmed hat. However, he did not let go of the reins.

'By the Holy Mother, Mickey Cohan!' yelled one of the half a dozen onlookers who were gathered around watching with obvious enjoyment. 'That's a real fine lesson you're teaching him, so it is!'

'The doing of it's just a mite hard on your bowler, though,' a second spectator called, employing another name by which the derby hat was known.

'Sure and he's not being what a man'd call respectful to you, Mickey!' mocked another of the men. 'And you the king snipe of our gang and all.'

Although they were empty handed, all the spectators were nearly as tall and brawny as the man they were watching. They were dressed in the same general fashion with the exception that their garments were somewhat cheaper in quality and inferior in cut and they had regained their headgear. Their voices implied that they too had Irish origins and, like him, they had clearly been drinking.

'Then it's making the evil bastard more respectful I'll be!' the bare headed man roared, his face becoming more suffused with rage as he looked down at the ruined hat. Stepping towards the burro, which had halted and was watching him warily, he raised the stick above his head, continuing, 'Hold this one, y – !'

Before the sentence could be completed, or the delivery of the intended blow could be commenced, the speaker heard fast moving footsteps approaching and profanely startled exclamations breaking from the onlookers. Then he felt the stick being grasped from behind and, although he tightened his hold, it was plucked from his hand as if he had not made the attempt.

'Ain't any call to go whomping the little feller with something *this* heavy, no matter what he's done,' a deep voice reproved, albeit in what seemed a mild tone, while the removal was taking place. 'It could easily kill him and I don't reckon, was you to calm down a mite, you'd want to do that.'

Such was the red haired man's surprise that the comment was delivered and he had been disarmed before he fully comprehended what was happening. On the realisation striking home, he gave vent to a bellowed profanity and released the reins. Paying no attention to the burro as it whirled and ran away, passing just as unheeded between two of the equally amazed spectators, he swung around wrathfully to find out who had had the temerity to intervene.

Having executed the turn, the burly red head's eyes widened almost as if he was unable to credit what he was seeing as he became aware of the way in which the interloper's bulk loomed over his far from diminutive frame. However, studying the apparently placid expression on the bearded giant's face and remembering the gentle, seemingly apologetic manner in which he had been addressed, he was less in awe than might otherwise have been the case. In fact, he fell into an error that others before him had made where Tiny Crumble was concerned.

Yet, even if Michael Cohan had given any thought to the discrepancy between their respective sizes, it was unlikely he would have allowed himself to be influenced on the side of discretion. Tact and caution were never his strongest points when he had been drinking. Furthermore, even if he had been sober, he would not have allowed the intervention to go unchallenged. He had acquired his well paid position as 'king snipe', section boss in charge of a band of railroad construction workers, as much by virtue of his fighting prowess as from a superior knowledge of, and ability at, the tasks they were required to perform. So he was aware that any hesitancy on his part, especially after his failure to ride or punish the burro, would be considered a sign of weakness by the watching gandy dancers and reduce his authority over them.

There was, the king snipe concluded, only one way to deal with the intrusion!

Knotting his left hand into a fist, Cohan swung it in the intruder's direction. The hard knuckles impacted against the side of the bearded jaw with considerable force. It was a good punch, thrown by a man with plenty of experience in such matters, but it produced surprisingly little effect. Although the recipient's head jerked and he was driven back a step, throwing aside the stick as he went, he neither fell nor even staggered. Yet the former, or at least the latter, had always happened on the numerous previous occasions when the gang boss had delivered a similar attack.

'I reckon you've got a right to be riled, mister,' the gigantic intruder said quietly, keeping his hands open and by his sides, as startled exclamations rose from the spectators. 'I shouldn't've billed in, only you looked like you was fit to bust that poor critter's head and I don't reckon's you'd've wanted to do no such thing had you thought on it a mite.'

In spite of the hunting and trapping of animals being his occupation, Tiny had a kind heart and hated to see needless cruelty inflicted upon any living creature. He had realised that his interference would almost certainly be resented, but he had been unable to prevent himself from going forward and stopping the enraged man continuing the attack upon the burro. Although the blow had not been light, he had no intention of retaliating. Instead, he was not only willing to let it pass without being returned, but had apologised in the hope of placating Cohan.

The hope did not materialise!

'I'll bust *your* god-damned head!' the gang boss bellowed, too angry to be mollified, lashing out with the other fist.

Landing just as hard on the bearded giant's chin, the second punch produced no more noticeable result than its predecessor. Having accepted it, he continued to step backwards without showing any sign of having felt it or of preparing to defend himself should the attack be continued.

Tiny's attempt to retreat without fighting met with no success!

Surprised, mortified and even a little alarmed by his failure to fell the bearded giant, Cohan essayed another blow with his left hand. It did not land. Accepting that his desire to avoid trouble was meeting with no success, Tiny brought up both his hands and caught the approaching fist before it could make contact.

Never had Cohan encountered such strength. Not only was his intended attack halted with an apparent ease which was close to frightening, his hand felt as if it was being crushed between the buffers of two railroad cars. The pain he was experiencing did not continue for very long, but he found its cessation gave him little relief. Impelled by a swinging heave which he was helpless to resist, he was swung in a half circle at an ever increasing speed around his pivoting captor. On being released, he hurtled with no control over his movements to collide with two of the watching gandy dancers and they all went down in a cursing heap.

After staring from their sprawled out companions to Tiny, the remaining gandy dancers exchanged glances. For all their amusement and comments over Cohan's misfortunes with the burro, he was no 'bear cat' as a bullying and unpopular gang boss was termed. There was more than just their liking for the 'king snipe' involved. They took the gravest exception to somebody intruding upon their affairs whose attire indicated he was not an employee of the railroad and might even be one of the greatly despised men involved in slaughtering buffalo for no more than the hides and tongues.

'Get the big, ugly, skin hunting bastard, lads!' yelled the largest of the quartet, as he bounded towards the bearded giant.

Although Tiny realised there was no acceptable way he could avoid having to protect himself, being aware of how easily his tremendous strength could cause him to inflict more serious injuries than he intended, he acted in what he considered to be the least dangerous manner. Employing a speed that was far from in keeping with his generally slothful behaviour, he laid the palm of his right hand on the face of the speaker and pushed. With the charge turned into an arm-flailing and rapid involuntary retreat, he repeated the shoving tactic with his left against the second would-be attacker to produce an identical result.

Taking a swift step to the right an instant later, the bearded giant caused the third gandy dancer to rush harmlessly by and, with a motion similar to swatting at a troublesome fly, hastened the departure with a swing of his right arm against the passing back. Driven onwards irresistibly, the man went sprawling winded and to his hands and knees. He landed a few feet from the back door of the saloon, close to where Cohan's stick had fallen.

Making the most of the fact that his companions were occupying Tiny's attention – although he was somewhat alarmed by the ease with which they were being disposed of – the fourth construction worker landed a punch to the side of the big man's head. It attained no greater success than those delivered by the gang boss and he was subjected to an even more spectacular reprisal. Before he could strike again, two enormous hands closed upon and bunched the front of his jacket. Lifted from his feet with no more apparent effort than if he had been a little child instead of a fully grown man, he was thrown backwards. On alighting at what seemed a remarkable distance from where he was released, he felt his left ankle buckle beneath him and collapsed with a yell of pain.

Rolling apart to the accompaniment of much profanity, Cohan and the two men he had felled scrambled back to their feet. Assisted by the pair who had been thrust aside, they returned to the attack. Fortunately for Tiny, they made no attempt to co-ordinate their efforts. In their mutual eagerness to repay the treatment they had received, they tended to impede rather than support one another. Still determined to avoid causing any more damage than was absolutely necessary, the bearded giant continued to defend himself without clenching his fists. Instead of punching, he displayed considerable speed and agility for one of his bulk, augmented by skill. He mostly concentrated upon deflecting the blows thrown at him while shoving or heaving his assailants away. On the occasions when he was compelled to strike one of them, he used either the flat palm or the back of his hand.

By the time the third man had regained the breath he had lost when he was sent sprawling, a glance to his rear informed him that his companions were meeting little success in their attempts to quell the buckskin clad interloper. Deciding more effective means than bare hands were called for, he noticed something close at hand which he considered would serve his purpose. So eager was he to put his idea into operation that, as he was reaching out, he paid no attention to the sound of the saloon's door being thrown open with some violence. Closing his fingers around the handle of the sturdy blackthorn walking stick, he saw a black boot descend to press both stick and hand firmly against the ground. The howl of pain he let out was mingled with running footsteps going past and a double clicking noise from closer at hand, but that was also beyond his immediate range of vision.

Restraining his inclination to take some form of action

against his assailant, the gandy dancer looked upwards and confirmed his suspicions with regards to the nature of the clicking. Pointing at his head and conveying the impression of being as large as the mouth of a railroad tunnel was the muzzle of a big revolver. Behind it stood a tall, lean figure dressed in all black Texas cowhand clothing, but with a dark and savage face more suited to an Indian brave on the warpath.

'You just leave it be and stay put, *hombre*!' commanded the menacing shape and it was almost a relief for the gandy dancer to hear the words spoken with a Texan's drawl.

Remembering his last visit to Mulrooney and combining that memory with the fact that the order had been issued in English, the man realised he was not being threatened by an Indian warrior intent on blowing off his scalp with a Dragon Colt instead of employing more conventional methods of collecting it. The appreciation provided him with only slight relief. Although the foot was removed from the stick, recognising his assailant as the Ysabel Kid, he decided against making anything which might be construed as a hostile gesture. A quick look in the direction of his companions informed him that, far from any of them being able to come to his assistance, they all had problems of their own. Accepting there was nothing he could do to improve their situation, he concluded his wisest course was to stay where he had fallen and hope nothing worse happened to him than having acquired a set of fingers which throbbed painfully. There was, he believed – being unaware of the changes in the town marshal's office – a likelihood of his party spending the remainder of Independence Day in gaol.

Studying the situation as they had emerged from the saloon, the two Texans and Frank Derringer had needed no discussion to help them select the most suitable line of action. Leaving the Kid to deal with the man nearest to the door, Mark Counter and the gambler had run towards the fight. Employing the kind of co-operation they had developed while serving as deputies, they separated and made their approach from different directions. Their tactics proved as effective as those being used by the Kid.

Sent in a twirling stagger by a shove from Tiny, the largest of the gandy dancers was just regaining control of his movements when he found himself confronted by Derringer. Or rather he saw ahead of him somebody who clearly did not belong to his party. Acting in what he considered to be a justifiable fashion, he threw a punch at a potential enemy.

Avoiding the fist which was coming his way with nimble precision, the gambler swung his cane in an almost horizontal arc. The device, a thin wooden sheath around the steel barrel and breech mechanism of a single-shot firearm, made a most effective club. Catching the man on his forward shin, it elicited a yelp of anguish and caused him to hop on the other leg while clutching at the point of impact with his hands. Nor did his difficulties end there. Brought around with a similar rapidity, the cane whacked across the seat of his pants. The impact destroyed his already disturbed equilibrium and toppled him to the ground.

Despite being empty handed and having the two fully loaded Army Colts in his holsters, Mark made no attempt to arm himself as he was approaching the conflict. What he could see happening informed him that there was no need to take such an extreme measure as drawing the guns. His estimation of the situation suggested that, providing the railroad workers were unaware that he was no longer a deputy and thought therefore that the original peace officers were helping Marshal Kail Beauregard to police the town on Independence Day, he might be able to terminate the conflict swiftly and without seeming to be siding with Tiny.

Arriving behind the remaining pair of gandy dancers, who were about to grab Tiny as he was delivering a backhand blow that knocked Cohan sprawling, the big Texan caught them by the scruffs of their necks and flung them in opposite directions. Having done so, hoping his intentions would not be misinterpreted, he leapt forward and enfolded the bearded giant in his arms.

'All right, big feller!' the blond giant snapped in an authoritative manner, feeling the enormous strength in the buckskin-covered arms as he was pinning them to Tiny's sides. 'Quit it right now, or you'll likely wind up in the pokey.'

'Whatever you say, *Mr Lawman*!' the big hunter responded, standing still immediately and justifying the Texan's faith in his quick wits. 'I'd sooner stay outside than spend the day sat in the gaolhouse.'

'The same goes for you railroad men!' Derringer supplemented, also realising what Mark was trying to do. Transferring the cane to his left hand while he was speaking, he drew and cocked his Army Colt with the right, continuing, 'The marshal told us he aims to have a quiet and peaceful Fourth of July.'

A feeling of consternation filled each of the men Mark had tackled as a realisation struck them of what the result of their action might be. As he had hoped, they had only returned to Mulrooney that morning and did not know he and the gambler were no longer peace officers. All they could think of was that, instead of spending the day celebrating, their party could be taken to gaol.

'Sure and wasn't that just what we was having, but for the skin hunter there?' protested the shorter of the pair, pointing a finger at the cause of their predicament. While aware of the completely fair and unbiased way in which the members of the town marshal's office always carried out their duties, he hoped the antipathy many Texans felt towards those engaged upon the wasteful work of shooting buffalo for the hides and tongues alone would lead the blond giant to discount any denial of his assertion. 'He jumped us for no reason at all!'

'That's the rights of it, Mr Counter, sir,' the second gandy dancer declared, trying to sound as if he was speaking the unvarnished truth. 'We was just going by here peaceful and – !'

'Oo, you bleeding pair of liars!' an irate voice accused, its mode of speech that of a working class Englishwoman who had – by tradition – been born within hearing distance of the bells of St Mary-le-Bow in Cheapside, London. 'You tell the truth, Mickey Cohan, or I'll make sure Miss Freddie never lets *any* of you set foot in the Fair Lady again.'

Small, buxom, young, blonde and very attractive, the speaker was stalking rather than merely walking from the alley at the end of the building. She was clad in the kind of plain black dress with long sleeves and a stiff white stand-up collar which was the accepted attire for one type of female domestic servant. Severe in line though the garment might have been intended to be, it was tailored to reduce that effect. The spotless frilly white apron over it emphasised her trim waist and a well developed bosom which was thrust forward in a manner indicative of righteous indignation and determination. Set on her piled up, curly hair, a small white cap shaped like the shell of an oyster had a jaunty look and would have complemented her pretty face if its normal good humour had not been replaced by lines of annoyance.

Shaking his head to clear the spinning sensation which was filling it and rubbing gingerly at his cheek, the gang boss let out his breath in a long sigh. Glancing around, he found that only one of his men showed signs of being injured. Having sobered considerably since the start of the fight, he could understand the implications of the discovery. Although the bearded giant was strong enough to have done a great deal of damage, he had refrained. Not many men would have shown such leniency under the circumstances. Gratitude for the consideration, mingled with an inborn sense of fair play and a sporting nature, told him there was only one honourable way to act. What was more, knowing the little blonde was capable of carrying out her threat, he had no desire to be barred from the best saloon in town and this was a further inducement.

'The boys've got the wrong of it, Mark,' Cohan admitted. 'It was us more than the big gent there who started it.'

'Well now,' Tiny injected. 'It wouldn't be right for me to let you gents take all the blame. I shouldn't've billed in the way I did.'

'What happened?' Mark asked, pleased with the bearded giant's comment and seeing the feeling was shared by the railroad workers.

'You know how it is when you've had a couple or more drinks,' Cohan explained, indicating a nearby building. 'I thought it'd be a joke to ride one of them donkeys that's for sale over at Willard's livery barn and I lost my temper when it threw me off. This gent stopped me beating the head off it with my stick and it's pleased I am that he did it.'

'Where's the burro now?' Mark inquired, glancing around.

'It run off when the fight started,' supplied the little blonde.

'Then I reckon *somebody* had best get it back,' Mark judged, and looked at the only man to have been injured. 'How bad hurt are you?'

'I think my ankle's broke,' the gandy dancer replied.

'Two of you take him to the doctor,' the blond giant commanded. 'And, was I the rest, I'd get that burro back before Willard finds out it's gone.'

'You crafty perisher, Mark Counter,' the girl said with a grin, after Cohan and his men had departed to carry out the tasks they were given. 'Making Mickey and his mates think you're still deputies.'

'We never *said* we were,' the blond giant pointed out. 'But having them think so made it a whole heap easier to calm them down than if they'd known Tiny was our *amigo*. Anyways, how come you're down this way, Babsy?'

'Miss Freddie and Cap'n Dusty sent me to find you,' the girl replied. 'I met Kail Beauregard and he told me where you were, but as Henry doesn't allow women in his place, I came round the back to get one of his blokes to fetch you out. Where's Waco?'

'Hasn't he been with you?' Mark inquired, pretending ignorance.

'You *know* he hasn't!' Babsy Buckingham asserted and swung a challenging glare at the other Texan. 'I suppose I'm a bloody fool for asking *you*, but where's he got to?'

'Now I wouldn't want to get *nobody* into trouble, mind,' the Kid drawled, in what sounded almost a tone of unctuous virtue. 'But, being raised to the truth-telling, I've got to admit I recollect he said something about dropping by to say, "Howdy, you-all," to that lil Ginger gal.'

'Why sure,' Derringer supported, as the little blonde turned an exasperated look his way. 'I seem to remember hearing him say something like that.'

'Seems I recollect he said he wasn't likely to be back any too quickly,' Mark went on. 'It takes time to say, "Howdy, you-all," to a gal the way – '

'*You* taught him,' the Kid interrupted.

At that moment, having compelled Julius Rickmansworth to carry the dead 'Mexican' to the marshal's office, the youngster being so cheerfully maligned by his companions was commencing his explanation of what had led to the shooting.

'Don't you lot give me any of *that*!' the little blonde yelped, having come to know the trio very well over the past few weeks. Adopting the attitude of a heroine in the kind of melodrama so popular at that period, she went on, 'He's too fine; too true; too loyal – and too scared of what I'd do to him if that was where he'd gone. Besides, after the licking I gave old Ginge', she wouldn't go mucking about with *my* bloke.'

'Well now,' the Kid grinned. 'Way I heard it, when you pair locked horns that time, it wound up a tie.'

'It *did,* but don't tell *her*, she *may* think I won,' Babsy replied, her expressive features showing amusement rather than shame as she thought of the fight – which had taken place during the battle royal that had culminated in the feud between the saloons owned by her employer and Buffalo Kate Gilgore – she had had with the red haired girl who was now her best friend.[1] 'Anyway, Ginge's been with me all morning, so you don't need to keep trying to drop the poor love in it. You're wanted down at the Fair Lady, Mark.'

'What's doing?' the blond giant inquired.

'One of the railroad bosses says he can get together a pretty strong bunch of blokes,' Babsy explained. 'So Miss Freddie said she'd get you to pick a team and give them a tug of war.'

'That's what she said, huh?' Mark drawled, glancing at Tiny and realising he was being presented with an excellent opportunity for delivering the invitation he had been discussing in the saloon. It was one which would reduce the chance of the bearded giant, who had proved to be far more perceptive than appeared on the surface, suspecting the real reason. 'Well now, I reckon we should ought to be able to accommodate them if that's what they have in mind.'

[1] The cause of the feud and how it was terminated is told in: *THE TROUBLE BUSTERS.* J.T.E.

CHAPTER NINE

I'LL TAKE IT OFF YOUR BODY

Watching the sombrely dressed man who was walking past his place of concealment and along the path through the clump of trees, Reg Wall concluded that at last his luck had taken a much needed turn for the better.

On regaining consciousness and finding himself alone in the alley, the pickpocket had assumed that the woman had gone to inform Marshal Kail Beauregard of the attempted robbery. Having no way of knowing how long it was since he had been rendered *hors-de-combat*, he had wasted no time in deciding what to do. Pausing only to pick up and holster his Navy Colt, he had set off with the intention of putting as much distance as possible between himself and what he believed to be a potentially dangerous area. Not until he was satisfied that he had evaded the deputies he felt sure would be sent to arrest him did he turn his attention to considering his future.

The first point to be settled by Wall as he sat in the shelter offered by a public toilet near the all but deserted cattle shipping pens alongside the railroad was that, now more than ever, it was imperative for him to acquire sufficient money to leave Mulrooney. Nor was he swayed solely by the memory of the instructions he had received from the Ysabel Kid. He felt sure that, being a competent peace officer, Beauregard would have obtained his description from the woman in case he eluded the deputies. Which suggested he would have to find some means other than the train to get out of the town, or make sufficient changes to his appearance to avoid recognition. Unless they located him before, a watch would be kept at the depot to prevent him getting aboard.

Such had been the pickpocket's perturbation over the predicament he imagined himself to be facing that he had forgotten the loot from his earlier and more satisfactory theft. At first, he was troubled by a vague recollection of having seen the pocketbook and handkerchief lying near his revolver while he was reaching for it. As they had not been in sight when he retrieved the weapon, he had assumed they had been carried off by the woman. Although it had been a relief to discover they were on his person, the thought that she had examined the book and replaced them never occurred to him. Instead, he had decided his memory was playing tricks.

Taking out and opening the pocketbook, Wall had been annoyed as he looked inside. While he was not illiterate, he had the greatest difficulty in reading anything other than print. So, unlike the woman, he was unable to decipher Oswald Nolly's handwriting. Nor, being disappointed at having ascertained it did not hold any money, had he the inclination to try. However, just as he was about to fling it in disgust into the cesspool below the seat, the sight of the red morocco binding struck a responsive chord in his memory.

There was, the pickpocket had realised, one place where he might be able to find the answer to his need for money. In fact, if he was lucky, he could also acquire a change of clothing. He wondered why he had not thought of it before, instead of contemplating a burglary.

Thrusting the pocketbook back where it had come from in an instinctive gesture, Wall had left the toilet and started at a brisk walk towards his destination. However, believing he was being sought by the peace officers, he had not chanced taking the most direct route. Such had been his caution that over an hour had elapsed before he had come to the well trodden path leading to Lily Gouch's 'Cathouse'. Although he had not been able to see the establishment, due to the path winding instead of taking a straight line through the clump of fairly dense woodland which ensured the privacy of the occupants and their customers, he could hear enough to indicate it was open and doing business.

Such had been the pickpocket's eagerness to arrive that he had come into sight of the small clearing in the centre of which the Cathouse was erected before he realised he was behaving in an impetuous and ill-advised fashion. His task was far from being a sinecure and it needed more planning than he had given it so far if he was to be successful. With that thought in mind, instead of crossing the clearing, he stepped behind a tree at the side of the track. Peering cautiously around the bulky trunk, he studied his surroundings and gave consideration to how he might best achieve his purpose.

Although nobody was in view, the sound of masculine laughter and voices assured the pickpocket there were potential victims within. However, past experience had taught him that he must not attempt his intended robbery on the premises. Being aware of how adversely she could be affected, Lily Gouch would never countenance such a thing happening to a customer under her roof. In fact, it was advisable that she should be kept in ignorance of any thefts perpetrated in her immediate vicinity for as long as possible. Fortunately, where the latter precaution was concerned, the nature of the surrounding terrain was in his favour. The only way of approaching and leaving the building was along the path and it had been cut in such a fashion that, shortly after the victim had left the clearing, he would be hidden from view on all sides by the woodland.

Having drawn the conclusion that picking the victim's pocket would no more serve his purpose under the present conditions than it would have with the woman, Wall had appreciated the value of the concealment from observation. Should he be seen employing the less subtle methods he was contemplating and was subsequently captured by Lily's bouncers, the consequences were likely to prove far more severe than if he was arrested by the local peace officers. Furthermore, he had wanted to ensure that whoever he selected would be unable to tell her what had happened until after he was safely beyond her reach.

The wait for a victim to appear had not been protracted. In fact, only about five minutes had elapsed before one put in an appearance.

Clad in a black suit, white shirt, a black necktie and the kind of 'stovepipe' hat favoured by undertakers, the man had come through the front door of the Cathouse. If such was his trade, studying his unsteady gait, Wall had concluded that he had not been called in by Lily Gouch to practise it. Rather, in addition to sampling the wares offered by her girls, he appeared to have been drinking. Halting at the edge of the porch, he glanced over his shoulder almost furtively. Then he reached into the left inside pocket of his jacket and took a wallet from it. Apparently he was afraid that he might have been robbed, for he opened it and counted the contents. Having satisfied himself that all was well, he returned the wallet and walked with weaving steps across the clearing.

Although Wall would have preferred to ambush a customer who was making for the Cathouse, he decided to make the most of the opportunity he was being offered. Not only did the man seem to be sufficiently drunk to make easy pickings, he still had a fair sum of money in his possession. What was more, they were close enough in size for his clothes to provide the disguise needed to evade the deputies at the railroad depot. Finally, his behaviour on leaving the building suggested he had not been in Mulrooney long enough to have learned of the strict code by which Lily operated. If he was a visitor in town for the Independence Day festivities, or to transact business, he might not be missed for a considerable time.

Allowing the man to go past his hiding place, the pickpocket glanced at the Cathouse to satisfy himself that nobody else was leaving, or watching. On setting out in pursuit, appreciating the necessity of ensuring the crime went unobserved, he did not hurry. The time to strike would be when they were out of sight of the building, but before they reached the other side of the woodland.

Bearing in mind how his attempt to rob the woman had failed, Wall was determined to avoid presenting his new intended victim with an opportunity to turn the tables on him. There was too much at stake for that. Instead of coming to grips, a blow to the back of the head with the butt of the Navy Colt would render the man unconscious. After he had been dragged into the concealment of the undergrowth, he could be searched and stripped of enough clothing to allow a complete change in his assailant's attire. With that done, he would be left bound hand and foot, with a gag in his mouth to prevent him from shouting for help when he recovered.

Providing everything was done properly, Wall believed there was a good chance of being well on his way to safety before anybody learned what had taken place.

Walking with great care, the pickpocket was alert for any

suggestion that the man was becoming aware of his presence. There was none. He continued to weave his unsteady way at the same pace and began to sing a popular ballad in a far from melodious voice with a Boston accent.

Wall regarded the vocalising with mixed feelings. While the extra noise reduced the chances of his approach being heard, its sudden cessation might be noticed and investigated by somebody from the Cathouse. So he decided to hold off his attack until they were almost at the other side of the woodland. Wanting to ensure that the man would see nothing suspicious if he should glance behind him, the pickpocket continued to keep his distance and refrained from drawing the Navy Colt.

Just after Wall concluded the time had come for him to make his move and increased his pace to close in, the man swerved towards the right side of the trail. For a moment, wondering if he had betrayed his intentions in some way, he was concerned. Then he decided this was not the case. Halting, but carrying on singing in – if anything – an even louder voice, the man leaned against the trunk of a tree with both hands in front of his body.

Satisfied that his intended victim was doing no more than answering the call of nature, Wall eased the Colt from its holster. Instead of keeping its butt in his hand and cocking the action, he grasped it around the frame to make it more effective as a club.

Step by stealthy step, the pickpocket advanced along the path!

Just three more strides were needed!

Then, having knocked off the stovepipe hat with the left hand, bringing down the Colt's butt with the right would be all that was required to obtain the means of leaving Mulrooney.

'Drop it, Wall!'

Whirling swiftly into the centre of the track as he was snarling out the command, there was every indication that the man had only been pretending to be under the influence of liquor. Certainly, as the fly of his trousers was fastened, he had not stopped for the reason envisaged by the pickpocket. He completed the turn, lining the short barrelled Colt Model of 1871 House Pistol in his right fist with disconcerting steadiness.[1] Cupped in the palm of his left hand, suggesting how he had known the attack was contemplated, he held a small pocket mirror.

'What the hell – ?' Wall gasped, so surprised and alarmed by the unexpected metamorphosis that he was incapable of doing anything more positive than freezing in his tracks.

'You heard me, you high diving son-of-a-bitch!' the Bostonian growled, making a menacing gesture with his weapon. 'Drop that gun!'

'All right, all right!' the pickpocket yelped and, realising that the way in which he was holding the Colt precluded any chance of using it as a firearm quickly enough to be able to defend himself, he dropped it to the ground in front of him. 'Take it easy, mister, I wasn't meaning any harm!'

'I'll just bet you weren't,' the man said drily and, returning the mirror to the side pocket of his jacket, he extended the left hand with its open palm upwards. 'Give it here.'

'Give *what* here?' Wall demanded, genuinely puzzled.

'The red pocketbook you lifted on Trail Street,' the Bostonian explained.

'What pocketbook?' Wall began in tones of well simulated indignation, his instinct to avoid making any admission of guilt causing him to speak before he had given thought to the implications of the demand.

'Don't come the innocent with me, you god-damned lousy fingersmith!' the man warned, advancing a stride, but halting just beyond reaching distance. 'I'll take it off your body if I have to!'

'Hey!' the pickpocket ejaculated, struck by the memory of what his victim had looked like. 'I didn't lift it off *you*!'

'Nobody said you did,' the man pointed out, glancing past Wall and making another threatening motion with his revolver. 'But I know the man it belongs to and he's madder than all hell over you taking it.'

By now, the pickpocket's mind was functioning rapidly and he was beginning to draw conclusions. The first was that he had clearly been wrong in regarding the pocketbook as almost worthless. Yet there had not been any money in it

[1] In spite of its name, the Colt Model of 1871 House Pistol was a four-shot revolver. Designed as a concealment weapon, the shape of its cylinder gave it an unofficial alternative name, the 'Cloverleaf'. J.T.E.

which could make the Bostonian insist upon its retrieval. Although the red morocco leather binding was expensive, that would hardly account for the pocketbook's value. All of which suggested that whatever was written inside must be the reason for its value. In which case, it deserved a closer examination than it had so far received.

The problem facing Wall was how to retain possession of his loot so he could look at it again. Denying all knowledge of it did not offer any solution. From what had been said, the man was aware both of his identity and of his proclivity for picking pockets. He had no need to ponder very long to realise how this had come about. The use of the terms, 'high diving' and 'fingersmith' implied that his intended victim had sufficient criminal connections to have obtained the requisite information.

'I threw it away when I found there wasn't any money in it,' Wall bluffed, more to gain time in which he could decide how to escape from his predicament than out of any hope that he would be believed.

'It'll go damned hard on you if you have!' the man declared, once again glancing along the trail towards the Cathouse as if wishing to make sure they were not being observed. 'Turn your pockets out and do it real careful!'

'All right, all right!' the pickpocket replied in tones of dejected resignation, struggling to conceal a sense close to elation over something he had just noticed about the condition of the weapon with which he was being covered. Reaching slowly into the appropriate pocket of his jacket with the left hand, he went on, 'Take it easy, mister. Here the son-of-a-bitch is.'

Producing and holding out the desired piece of his loot, Wall released it an instant before it could be taken from him. As he hoped would happen, the man's gaze followed it downwards and the barrel of the revolver wavered from its alignment. Making a grab before the weapon could be turned back towards him, he caught hold of the black sleeved arm with both hands. Eager as he was to gain control of the situation, the act was not caused by reckless desperation. Having observed that the action of the Colt was not cocked, he had known he could make the grab with comparative safety provided he first created a distraction.

Although a startled exclamation broke from the Bostonian, he did not allow himself to be disarmed. Catching Wall's right wrist with his free hand, he tried to liberate himself. Holding on grimly, the pickpocket became aware that somebody was approaching rapidly from behind him. Glancing over his shoulder, he discovered to his consternation that a fairly tall, burly man was almost within reaching distance.

Clad in a derby hat, cheap town suit, shirt and necktie, the newcomer's somewhat sallow and Mongoloid features suggested Baltic origins. Even though nothing was said, he clearly had no doubts over who to support. Swinging up his right hand, he lashed out savagely with the leather wrapped, spring-loaded sap he was grasping.

Having been in such a hurry to flee from the alley, Wall had not delayed to pick up his *kepi*. So he did not have even the slight protection it would have offered. Struck on the top of the head with considerable force, he collapsed instantly and as if he had been boned. Showing considerable dexterity, the man struck at him again as he was going down. He did not feel the second blow, the first having already done so much damage he was unconscious.

'You left it late enough, Miskie!' the Bostonian complained, delivering an unnecessary kick to the ribs of the sprawled out, motionless pickpocket.

'God-damn it, 'Digger, I done just what you told me to!' the newcomer protested indignantly, giving not so much as a single glance at the victim of his vicious attack. He spoke English with an intonation which suggested he had spent the majority of his life in the less salubrious districts of New York's East Side. 'You said's how *you'd* get him to come after you and, once he was out of sight of the Cathouse, I should sneak up so's he wouldn't know I was after him. And that's what I did.'

'That's what you did, all right,' the Bostonian conceded. He was aware of how uncertain Boris Miscowitz's temper could be and he had no wish to cause it to be turned upon him. So he continued, hoping to apply a soothing touch, 'You've got to hand it to Ossie, though. He called the tune right when he said we should come to the Cathouse.'

Meeting the rest of his gang as they were setting out to obey the instructions delivered by Charlotte Solikin, Oswald

Nolly had told them of the conversation he had overheard at Henry's Saloon. Such were the powerful associates upon whom he could call that, on their arrival at the Last Chance Casino, Gustav Folbert had had no hesitation in supplying the information demanded. Learning that the man they were seeking was in dire financial straits, Nolly had demonstrated a flair for deductive reasoning that many a peace officer would have envied.

Claiming that Wall would be unlikely to chance picking pockets on the streets after having received the warning from the Ysabel Kid, Nolly had guessed his need for money to leave town would cause him to try elsewhere and by other means. So he had told Miscowitz and Arnold 'Gravedigger' Kilburn to go to Lily Gouch's Cathouse and make inquiries.

Fortune had favoured the pair. While they were questioning one of the bouncers, they had seen and, aided by a description obtained from Folbert, recognised the man they were seeking as he was approaching along the path. Watching him take cover behind a tree instead of crossing the clearing to the building, Kilburn had guessed what he was meaning to do. Waiting until the bouncer – who had not noticed the pickpocket – left them, he had outlined a scheme by which he hoped they would regain possession of the pocketbook. By presenting himself as a drunken and worthwhile victim, relying upon the mirror to keep him informed of the danger, he had been successful in luring Wall into their clutches and had achieved their purpose.

'Yeah and he'll not be slow in telling us he did,' Miscowitz asserted, filled with the envious bitterness of a poorly educated and far from quick witted person for one who was more brilliant and who frequently pointed out the shortcomings of those less favoured. Then, pointing down, he went on, 'Is that the book he had lifted?'

'That's the one,' Kilburn confirmed, returning the Colt to its place of concealment under the left side of his jacket before picking up and pocketing the object in question.

'Do you reckon this bastard's read what's in it?' Miscowitz inquired, indicating Wall with a negligent wave of his sap-filled right hand.

'It doesn't matter a whole heap whether he did or not,' Kilburn stated, after making a quick examination of the pickpocket's unresisting body. 'He's not going to be able to talk about it.'

'I croaked him, huh?' Miscowitz grunted, showing neither remorse nor concern over the possibility.

'He didn't die of old age,' Kilburn said, with no greater display of emotion. 'Haul him off the track and make sure he won't be found in a hurry.'

'Sure, 'Digger,' the burly man assented. 'It looks like there's nothing to stop us going ahead now.'

'*He's* not, that's for sure,' Kilburn admitted. 'But we've still got to find a way of getting into the office.'

CHAPTER TEN

I'M RELYING UPON YOU-ALL

'Heave!' screamed Babsy Buckingham, the word being echoed by the equally excited crowd of spectators gathered behind the Fair Lady Saloon. 'Heave!'

Grasping the thick rope in both hands, Mark Counter leaned back and spiked the high heels of his cowhand boots more firmly into the ground. In front of the blond giant, Dusty Fog and Tiny Crumble were doing the same, although the latter's moccasins did not offer such a good purchase. For all that, the three of them were achieving at least some of their purpose. At the other end of the rope, the eight men selected as their opponents in the tug of war were straining with considerable vigour and were having no success in compelling them to move forward. However, as yet, neither were they able to haul their opponents across the line gouged in the soil at the half way point.

Regardless of the tremendous amount of effort he was being called upon to expend, the bearded giant was enjoying himself far more than he had believed would be the case when he left home. The fight with the railroad construction workers had had a far better outcome than he expected from past experiences. Furthermore, particularly since his arrival at the Fair Lady Saloon, he had been accorded a friendship and respect he found both pleasant and satisfying. It was vastly different to the treatment to which he had almost invariably been subjected on visits to other towns.

All too conscious of his lack of the social graces, Tiny had had qualms as he was being taken to meet Freddie Woods. Having been informed while on his way there that she not only operated the best saloon, but had been a major influence in Mulrooney acquiring its excellent reputation, he had expected to be confronted by a middle-aged dragoness with a domineering mien and attitude. This was far from being the case. Not much older than Babsy, she was black haired, radiantly beautiful and had a magnificently endowed figure which her elegant dress neither sought to flaunt nor hide.

Tiny's next fear, that – being a member of the English aristocracy,[1] according to the little blonde who clearly idolised her – Freddie would regard him as an uncouth and graceless country bumpkin had proved equally groundless. Not only had she quickly put him completely at his ease, but on being informed by Mark of his predicament, she had immediately offered him accommodation. When she had apologised because this would have to be in the empty liquor store behind the bar, due to the number of other guests she already had on the premises, he had declared he would be happy to make use of it and was told to leave his rifle and pack in it until arrangement could be made for him to meet a possible purchaser of his skins.

On being introduced to Dusty Fog, Tiny had received one of the greatest surprises of his life.

After all he had heard regarding the already legendary young Texan's prowess in various fields,[2] the bearded giant had envisaged a man even taller and more muscular than Mark Counter. This had proved far from correct. Dusty was not quite five foot six in height. He had dusty blond hair and his tanned features, while moderately good looking, were far from as eye-catching as those of Mark or the Ysabel Kid. Nor did he appear to be anywhere near so well dressed as might be expected from one of his importance. Although he was wearing clothing of excellent quality and cut, he conveyed the impression that they were somebody else's cast-offs.

However, for all the Rio Hondo gun wizard's apparently diminutive build and seemingly nondescript appearance, the

[1] 'Freddie Woods' was born Lady Winifred Besgrove-Woodstole and subsequently married Dusty Fog. However, on being asked by the author, their grandson, Alvin Dustine 'Cap' Fog, declined to supply any information regarding her reasons for leaving England and settling in the United States. J.T.E.

[2] For the benefit of new readers: details of Dusty Fog's career and special qualifications are given in: *APPENDIX ONE* J.T.E.

bearded giant had not been long in his company before he grew aware of his commanding presence. Small he undoubtedly was, in comparison with most of those around him, but such was the strength of his personality that it transcended his lack of feet and inches. Another point had struck Tiny when he looked closer. While the small Texan's attire tended to conceal rather than exhibit the fact, he was far from being puny in build.

Visual proof of the latter had been provided in no uncertain manner!

In addition to noticing that Tiny was on good terms with the Floating Outfit boys, news of his and Mark's exploit outside Henry's Saloon had caused him to be the subject of much interest and speculation among the other customers. As the afternoon had worn on, there had been considerable friendly discussion over just how strong the two big men would be in combination. This had come to a head with the arrival of the eight men selected by a prominent railroad official to compete in the tug of war. Pointing out how the pair had lifted the wagon unaided, he had suggested that they alone should take on his team. As their sponsor, Freddie had declined and insisted they must have at least a third puller on their side and this was agreed upon by the committee appointed as referees.

At first, Tiny had been somewhat surprised at Mark's choice of Dusty as the third member of their attenuated team when so many larger and heavier men were available.[3] The reason had become obvious as soon as the small Texan had removed his jacket, neck-tie and shirt. Doing so had exposed his torso, displaying very wide shoulders and a slender waist, to confirm Tiny's earlier assumption that he had a much better build than was discernible when he was fully clothed. Such was his muscular development that, if they had been the same height, proportionately it would be slightly greater than that of the blond giant.

Tiny had soon realised that his own lack of knowledge and experience had been another reason for Mark's choice. Whereas he had neither participated in, nor even seen, a tug

[3] Another occasion when, being required to carry out a task demanding exceptional physical strength, Mark Counter selected Dusty Fog to assist him is described in: *THE PEACEMAKERS*. J.T.E.

of war, the same did not apply to Dusty. From what had been said, the two Texans had teamed up in the past. He had discovered that such a contest entailed more than just taking hold and pulling on the rope. Drawing upon the lessons they had learned in previous competitions, they had described the tactics they intended to employ and, with the willing agreement of their opponents, had shown him how he could best help them.

When satisfied that the bearded giant knew the rudiments of the contest, the two teams had gone behind the saloon to commence. With the exception of the 'barmaids', as Tiny had been informed the three buxom women serving behind the counter were known, everybody who was in the barroom had accompanied them. Furthermore, as word of what was to take place had been widely circulated, people had congregated from elsewhere and a fair crowd of spectators had assembled.

After the formalities had been completed, the two Texans and Tiny had taken their positions on the rope and their opponents grasped the other end. Having made sure that the centre of the three pieces of white rag tied around it was directly over the mark carved in the ground by the Ysabel Kid's bowie knife, Freddie had given the signal for the tug of war to commence. With Babsy – who had changed from her maid's attire into the more revealing costume of a saloon-girl – acting as their vocal and very enthusiastic coach, the trio had begun to resist the strain which was being applied by the eight brawny men.

Almost five minutes had gone by.

In spite of never having taken part in such an event, after a momentary awkwardness, the bearded giant had soon proved he was worthy of his place on the team. Years of experience in making use of his weight and strength for various purposes had taught him how they could best be utilised even in such an unfamiliar situation. While the trio had not met with any success so far as achieving their ultimate goal was concerned, neither had they been compelled to move as much as a step forward.

'Come on now, you fellers!' called the railroad official, in his capacity of coach for his team. 'Stop just standing there and get to hauling them over the line!'

'Hot damn, boss, *that's* what we're trying to do!' the beefy captain of the team protested, with equal good humour, through gritted teeth. 'It's them three ornery cusses's just won't budge one way or the other!'

Another member of the crowd was growing impatient with the lack of motion, but regarded it in a far less amiable fashion.

Having been informed that his pocketbook was recovered and the thief who had stolen it was dead, Oswald Nolly had set out to attend to the interrupted part of his plan. Learning where Tiny had gone on his arrival at Henry's Saloon, he had followed and remained at the Fair Lady. Although he had not found an opportunity to make contact, nothing he had seen or heard had led him to assume he was incorrect with his summation of the bearded giant's mentality.

However, looking at his watch, the Bostonian was growing worried by the thought of how much of the day had passed. Information had reached him which made it imperative for his scheme to be perpetrated that night. This meant his time was restricted and he must establish before much longer whether the big man would serve his purpose. If the answer was in the negative, he would have to try and find some other means of attaining his goal.

'Did you-all hear that gent, Babsy-gal?' the Kid inquired. 'Why I'm mortal 'shamed of you. Now you straight off stop them shiftless loafers standing around and get 'em to doing *something*.'

'I'd try biting them on the leg was I you-all, Babsy,' Waco advised. 'Only do it from the *front*, so's they goes *backwards*.'

'I'll bite *you* on the bleeding leg if you don't belt up!' the little blonde threatened breathlessly, having expended a tremendous amount of energy in exhorting and encouraging the three men she was coaching.

'Oh please do try, Mr Counter, for *my* sake!' requested a feminine voice, its drawling intonation that of a well educated Southerner, after the laughter provoked by Babsy's spirited response died away. 'I've wagered a whole *two* dollars and I'm relying upon you-all to make sure I don't lose. In fact, proper or not, I'll give each of you a kiss when you win.'

'You hear that now, Dusty, Tiny?' Mark demanded,

having darted a glance at the speaker, as he leaned backwards with the end of the rope under his right arm, across his back, over the left shoulder, underneath the left arm and around him again for added security and leverage.

'It's a better offer than we've had so far,' the small Texan replied, without taking his eyes from the leading man of the other team.

'And it wouldn't be right to disappoint a lady!' Tiny went on. 'So how's about it. Are you fellers set to do more'n just stand?'

'I've been set ever since we started,' Dusty asserted, although – like his two larger teammates – the expression on his face, the freely flowing perspiration and the way he was speaking gave evidence of the tremendous effort that was required just to remain where they had been positioned at the start of the tug of war. 'So what're we going to do about it?'

'Well now,' Mark answered. 'I'd say it's about time we started hauling instead of just standing.'

'Let's get to doing it then!' Tiny suggested.

Having carried out their brief exchange of comments, which were greeted by yells of amused approval from the spectators, the two Texans and the bearded giant turned all their attention to expending even more of their combined weight and strength to pulling.

So did the eight men at the other end of the rope!

Interested though he might be in watching the efforts of his *amigos*, having taken an instant liking to and included the bearded newcomer in that category on their being introduced, Waco had nevertheless turned his gaze to the woman who had requested help so she could win her bet. Something about her voice had struck a vaguely responsive chord in his memory. However, even on locating her, he was unable to decide exactly what it might be. Nor, while he was positive he would not have forgotten any previous meeting, did he recognise her.

Standing at the forefront of the crowd, although she had not been there while the preliminaries of the tug of war were taking place, the speaker was such a magnificent example of her sex that the young Texan felt no surprise over discovering the predominantly masculine spectators had permitted her to attain such a favourable position. In fact, loyal as he was to those he liked, he was willing to concede she ran Freddie a very close second in looks, poise, charm and elegant demeanour.

Matching the lady saloonkeeper in height and build, the woman looked to be about the same age. A blonde, her hair was neatly coiffured in the Cadogan style and she did not wear a hat. The rich tan of her beautiful face, which had lines indicative of a strong personality, suggested much of her life was spent out of doors. She was tastefully dressed in an expensive fawn two-piece travelling costume. If less sedately daring than Freddie's formal black silk gown, it was equally flattering to her figure. There were no rings on her fingers. Her right hand was grasping the neck of a somewhat larger than usual black satin vanity bag which dangled from her wrist.

One of Waco's predominant character traits, which he had been encouraged by Dusty to exercise while he was serving as a deputy town marshal, was his insatiable curiosity. Whenever something aroused his interest, his instinct was to try and learn more. However, on this occasion, he was diverted before he could reach any conclusions where the woman was concerned. Wanting to give vocal support to his three *amigos*, he turned his attention back in their direction and joined vigorously in the encouragement they were receiving at Babsy's instigation.

For almost five minutes, in spite of the clamour being raised by the spectators, the situation appeared to remain static. While none of the opposing team could match Mark or Tiny in sheer size and bulk, not one could be considered puny. For all that, try as they might, they were unable to draw the two Texans and the bearded giant forward. Instead, slowly yet inexorably, and all their efforts to resist notwithstanding, they began to be subjected to exactly the opposite effect.

Inch by contested inch, no matter how much they leaned back and tried to resist, the eight men found themselves being dragged after the retreating trio. Not one of them, nor more than a few of the crowd for that matter, realised why this was happening. It went beyond the fact that they lacked the co-ordination of their opponents. In addition to possessing Herculean strength, the small Texan and the blond giant had another major advantage over the railroad workers. Because of the nature of their employment, their footwear was more suitable to the task upon which they were engaged.

The boots worn by Dusty and Mark had been made by Joe Gaylin, the old master leatherworker of El Paso, with the specialised needs of a working cowhand in mind. Resisting the determined efforts of a horse, cow, steer or bull to escape after it had been roped while on foot called for a secure hold to be retained upon the ground. It also served as excellent training for participating in a tug of war. Having taken such rugged usage into account, it was Gaylin's boast that nothing could rip the heels from any pair of boots he manufactured. The tremendous strain to which those of the two Texans were being subjected was proving the claim was justified.

At last, to the accompaniment of tumultuous applause even on the part of those spectators who had made losing wagers, the piece of white rag fastened on the railroad team's side of the rope passed over the mark on the ground. Watching for this to happen, in her capacity as judge, Freddie signified that the Texans and the bearded giant were the winners.

'And not before time, I might add!' the lady saloonkeeper continued, glancing at the position of the sun with regards to the western horizon. 'I thought we were going to be kept waiting here all night before something happened.'

'Shucks now, Miss Freddie,' protested the captain of the losing team, soaked with perspiration and gasping out the words, but clearly far from disgruntled by the defeat. 'If you'd only've said something sooner, we'd've let them win afore now.'

'I'm *sure* you would,' the Englishwoman replied. 'Now let's get back inside. The first drink for everybody is on the house.'

'Hey now!' chuckled another perspiring, but equally cheerful railroad worker, as he flexed his stiff fingers. 'Had we knowed you was going to say that, we'd've got through as soon as we started.'

'Or even sooner,' a third competitor asserted, then nodded to where the beautiful blonde was walking forward. 'And if she'd've offered to give me a kiss for winning, I'd've done it myself.'

Also watching the woman as she was carrying out the promise she had made, Waco noticed there was a distinct difference in the way she treated the recipients. While Dusty and Tiny were given no more than a quick peck on the cheek such as might have been delivered by a sister, Mark received a kiss full on the lips.

There was, the youngster decided, nothing sisterly about the blond giant's reward.

'Hey, Lon,' Waco said, turning to his black dressed companion who was gazing at the blonde and Mark. 'Do you know that gal?'

'Well now,' the Kid answered. 'I couldn't say right out what her name might be, but I reckon I've seen her some place or another.'

'So's Mark, way they're taking on,' the youngster commented, as the blond giant took the young woman by the hand and started to walk with her towards the rear entrance of the saloon. 'Fact being, I'd say he knows her pretty good.'

'He knows a whole heap of pretty gals right good,' the Kid pointed out.

'Why do I get the sneaky notion *you* know a whole heap more'n you're telling?' Waco demanded, studying his companion's seemingly innocent face with suspicion.

'That's cause you've been going around with a certain tinhorn gambler so much you've got all distrustful of folks,' the Kid claimed, nodding to Frank Derringer as if to ensure the youngster was left in no doubt as to whom he was referring. 'Anyways, let's go and get us our drink on the house. Happen Mark'll overlook what an ornery cuss you've got to be and'll present you to the lady after we've had it.'

On the point of returning to the barroom, Nolly felt a hand on his sleeve. Instantly, remembering how he had lost the pocketbook earlier in the day, he swung around to ensure that whoever was accosting him did not have something similar in mind.

'That was really something to see,' Charlotte Solikin remarked. She had arrived while the tug of war was taking place, but had been unable to reach the Bostonian until the other spectators had started to disperse.

'It was indeed, my dove,' Nolly agreed. 'In fact, the more I see of him, the greater grows my conviction that yonder over-sized country bumpkin fulfils the requirements of our needs.'

'Have you got to him yet?' the girl inquired.

'As yet, no,' Nolly confessed.

'The boys are getting edgy,' Charlotte warned. 'That's why I told them I'd come and find out what's happening.'

'Patience is a virtue, my little rose blossom,' the stocky man stated, being aware that the girl shared his male associate's lack of that quality. 'And it would behove all of you to cultivate it.'

'That's all very well for you to say,' Charlotte answered. 'But if we don't – !'

'I have not the slightest need to be informed of the disastrous effect an extensive delay would have upon our scheme, my impetuous flower,' Nolly declared. 'Yet I am also and equally cognisant of the perils which might appertain to undue haste.'

'Well then – !' Charlotte commenced, just a trifle nervously as she had detected the hardening of her companion's voice and knew his temper was wearing thin.

'It is imperative that *nobody* connects the bumpkin with us,' Nolly pointed out. 'But have no fear, I am alert for the earliest opportunity to make his acquaintance unobserved and will seize it the instant it presents itself. In the meantime, you can return to our impatient associates and ensure they know what I require of them when I bring him with me.'

'I'd do it,' Charlotte declared. 'But you haven't got around to telling me what you *have* got in mind.'

'Is that all clear?' Nolly demanded, after he had explained to the girl what she would be required to do. Receiving a nod of agreement, he went on, 'Off you go then and await his coming, my dove. Have no fear, I will deliver the hayseed suitably prepared to be led like a lamb to slaughter.'

CHAPTER ELEVEN

I JUST *KNOW* YOU CAN BE TRUSTED

'Come in, my good sir,' Oswald Nolly said, glancing at the bulky pack carried by Tiny Crumble. He also noticed that, although the bearded man was a little flushed under his tan, his visitor showed no sign of being drunk. 'Come in, I'm delighted to see you have decided to avail yourself of my invitation.'

Moving aside to let the big man walk in, the Bostonian looked first right and then left along the second floor passage of the Railroad House Hotel. There was nobody in sight, for which he was grateful, but he received a quick wave of Charlotte Solikin's right hand from the door of the next room which was slightly ajar as he was turning to follow his visitor. The girl's signal had informed him that she was aware of who had arrived and that she was ready to play the part which he had assigned to her. Relief mingled with the satisfaction he felt on closing his own door. Although they still had to persuade the bearded giant to render assistance, he was confident this could be achieved without too much difficulty.

There was good cause for Nolly to feel relieved.

After having sent Charlotte to deliver his instructions, Nolly had joined the crowd in the barroom of the Fair Lady Saloon. However, it was not until almost ten o'clock that he had been able to contact Tiny with sufficient privacy for his purpose. While he was waiting, the arrival of first one and then another of his other male associates had warned him that they were growing increasingly concerned over the delay. Despite the mounting pressure to which he had been subjected, he had refused to be rushed and, in the end, his patience had been rewarded.

Following the bearded giant into the men's restroom and

satisfying himself that it had no other occupants, Nolly had opened the conversation along the lines which his knowledge about his intended victim had suggested would prove most fruitful. Introducing himself as a buyer of furs and hides from the East, he had claimed to be distressed at having learned that the prices he was charged by the local dealers were far higher than those they paid to the hunters. Considering this unfair, it was his intention to cut out the grasping middlemen provided he could obtain his supply direct. He had then expressed his 'surprise' on being informed that the man he was addressing was not only a hunter, but harboured similar suspicions with regards to the dealers.

Knowing that somebody might come into the restroom at any moment and wanting to avoid having his connection with the bearded giant known, the Bostonian had suggested they went outside to talk in private. When this had been done, he had offered to examine the other's furs with a view to making a bid for them. He had also warned that the negotiations must be conducted in secrecy as it would prove most embarrassing for Freddie Woods if the local dealers heard that an arrangement had been originated on her premises which could endanger their profits. Agreeing such a thing must be avoided at all cost, Tiny had accepted the proposal that he should collect his furs without anybody else knowing and deliver them to his 'benefactor's' room at the Railroad House Hotel. He had then been given instructions for making his arrival without going through the entrance lobby and being seen by the desk clerk.

Having done all he could on the spot, Nolly had – he hoped only temporarily – parted company with his intended dupe. Although the other had returned to the saloon, he was satisfied that he had prevented any reference being made to what had passed between them. Tiny had been vehement in his declaration that he would not do anything which might have an adverse effect upon his hostess and he was the kind of man who could be counted upon to keep his word. Nor did the Bostonian doubt he would come to the hotel in the manner which had been suggested to him.

For all his confidence that he had persuaded their dupe to do as he wished, at least as far as paying the visit went, Nolly had experienced some qualms on rejoining the other members of the gang. Studying their attitudes of thinly veiled hostility, he had known he would be finished as their leader if he failed to keep the other promise he had made. They would never forgive him if the profits they were anticipating should fail to materialise. Nor would the matter end there. His inability to carry out the robbery which had brought them to Mulrooney – regarded by all of them as a hick town in the wilderness – would seriously damage his standing in Eastern criminal circles and would make it difficult for him to obtain suitable assistants in the future.

Being aware of the consequences, despite having put on an air of assurance while sending his associates to carry out their various duties, Nolly had been extremely anxious until a knock had heralded the arrival of the bearded giant and he had been able to bang on the wall to notify the occupants of the next room that things were going as he had said they would.

'Take a seat, my good sir,' the Bostonian instructed, watching his visitor putting the pack on the floor by the bed. 'I trust you experienced not the slightest difficulty in reaching my temporary abode?'

'Nope,' Tiny replied, gazing around the luxuriously furnished room with something close to awe. Crossing to the only chair, by the dressing table, he lowered himself on to it cautiously, hoping it would support his weight. 'I done just what you said and come through the door in the alley, then made sure nobody was about afore I snuck up the stairs.'

'And, of course, you ensured that *nobody* saw you bringing your wares from the saloon?'

'I made good and sure.'

'You made no mention of our intended negotiations to *anyone*?'

'Not even to Mark, nor Cap'n Dusty,' Tiny affirmed, looking uncomfortable. 'I just said's how I wasn't used to late nights 'n' fancy doings, so I reckoned I'd go and bed down for a spell.'

'Such secrecy was, as I pointed out, a regrettable, but most necessary precaution, my good sir,' Nolly declared, being disturbed by the bearded giant's attitude. 'Like yourself, I have the greatest respect and admiration for Miss Woods. It would ill become us to in any way be the cause of possible embarrassment and hostility for so fine and charming a lady.'

'I'm not gainsaying *that*,' Tiny stated. 'It's just that I hope they don't take offence when they hear I snuck out the way I did.'

The bearded giant was ill at ease!

But not for the reasons which were worrying the Bostonian criminal!

Possessing an honest and straightforward nature, Tiny was perturbed by thoughts of the subterfuge he had employed to leave the Fair Lady Saloon, not because he was suspicious.

Even though the bearded giant believed he was acting with the best of motives, he was unable to hold back the pangs of conscience caused by knowing he had lied to people who had shown him so much consideration, kindness and friendship. Nor could he draw any great consolation from telling himself he had at least told part of the truth when making his excuses. Except when he was out hunting, he was rarely up late at night. However, despite the exertions of the day, he had been enjoying himself and had found everything too interesting to feel tired and in need of rest.

Although he had not thought of the matter, the enjoyment could have provided another sop for Tiny's conscience. In spite of everybody behaving in such a friendly manner, and even because of it, his financial straits had begun to make him feel out of place. It had gone beyond the fact that the Texans and Frank Derringer had each had a female companion. He had had the opportunity to do the same, but – having found the girls far different from the rough and uncouth variety with whom circumstances usually caused him to associate – even though the subject had not been mentioned by anybody, he had considered his shortage of money would not allow him to entertain a lady. So he should have been pleased to tell what was no more than a white lie, and thus save himself from possible financial embarrassment.

'Have not the slightest apprehension upon that account, my good sir!' Nolly boomed jovially, realising with relief that his concern was groundless and that the big man was not suspicious of him. Despite knowing that the successful outcome of his scheme would preclude the other from passing on the information, he continued, 'When you return at the conclusion of what I'm confident will be a fruitful negotiation, you can tell them, in the strictest confidence, of course, why you felt the need for the subterfuge and, if you wish, lay the blame for it upon me. No, sir, more than that, I will accompany you and explain myself.'

'Thats' right good of you,' Tiny said. 'Tell you the truth, I've been worrying about not having enough money to set up drinks in my turn and selling you my furs'll let me do it tonight instead of having to wait until tomorrow.'

'Assuredly it will, sir,' Nolly agreed, glancing at the door.

'Shall I open up my pack and let you look at 'em?' Tiny inquired, starting to rise.

'Perhaps you would care for a drink first, sir?' Nolly countered, having no desire to take the chance of his ignorance of furs being made known to the bearded giant. He also wanted to delay until Charlotte arrived.

'I'd sooner not, happen that's all right with you,' Tiny refused mildly and apologetically. 'Never was much of a drinking man myself and I've already had my fill down to the saloon.'

'So be it, sir,' Nolly assented, with an amiability he was far from feeling. 'I've always had the greatest admiration for a man who knows when to say "no".'

'I'll open her up then,' the bearded giant offered, relieved by the ready acquiescence. 'And I'll buy *you* one when we get back to the Fair Lady.'

One of the many things which Tiny had liked about the Texans and the gambler had been their attitude to drinking. Knowing he had a poor head for liquor and hating the sensations caused by over indulgence, he had had qualms over the prospect of celebrating in their company. Much to his satisfaction, they had stuck to beer and, as their preferences on the subject were clearly known to all the other customers, neither they nor he had been pressed to take anything stronger.

However, experiences in the past had taught the bearded giant that a refusal – no matter how justified – could cause offence and he had been worried in case his rejection would put in jeopardy the business he had come to conduct. The apparently friendly and unhesitating way in which his decision had been accepted strengthened his belief that, for all his pompous speaking, the Easterner was a man who could be trusted. Which was exactly why Nolly had behaved the way he had.

Before Tiny could do more than walk across to his pack, the door flew open. Swivelling around with his right hand going to the hilt of the bowie knife, he refrained from drawing it when he saw who was coming into the room. While he did not recognise the newcomer, he felt there was no cause for alarm.

Leaving the male member of the gang who had stayed with her to await the outcome, Charlotte had arrived to play her part in the intended deception. Although the hood of the long black cloak she was wearing hung back to display her hair and beautiful face, it was fastened in such a way that it hid the garments beneath it. Her attitude suggested she was distressed.

'Uncle Ossie!' the girl gasped. 'I've just come from Brother Terry. He's got himself into trouble ag – '! Bringing the words to a halt, she stared at the bearded giant as if she had just become aware of his presence. Fluttering her left hand to her mouth, she went on, 'Oh heavens! I didn't know you had a visitor.'

'Don't go, my dear,' Nolly said solicitously, as Charlotte made as if to withdraw through the door she had left open. 'What's wrong?'

'I – I'd rather not say in front of a stranger,' the girl objected, but refrained from leaving.

'Have no fear on that account, my dear,' Nolly instructed, oozing confidence and waving a hand towards his intended dupe. 'I am certain we can rely upon Mr Crumble as a man of great discretion. Be assured he would *never* contemplate speaking of anything he overhears. Can we not count upon it, my good sir?'

'You certain sure can, ma'am!' Tiny promised emphatically, but started to walk across the room. 'Anyways, I can right easy go and wait outside if – !'

'Why that *won't* be necessary, sir,' Charlotte declared, directing what appeared to be a grateful and innocent look of admiration at the bearded giant. 'Anybody can see *you are* a perfect *gentleman* and I just know you can be trusted.'

'But – !' Tiny began, flattered and a little flustered by

what he believed to be the girl's genuine sincerity and approbation.

'Why I'd be mortified if I thought a friend of Uncle Ossie left because he was under the impression that I felt he wasn't trustworthy,' Charlotte stated, seeming distressed by the possibility, but without appearing bombastic. 'Truly *mortified*.'

'It's not that way at all, ma'am,' Tiny asserted hurriedly, the basic gallantry of his nature recoiling from the suggestion that he had hurt the feelings of the beautiful and, apparently, very perturbed young woman. 'I just thought – !'

'Please don't go, sir,' Charlotte begged, exuding what past experience had taught her would be taken for pathetic eagerness. Reaching behind her, she gave the door a push which closed it and went on, 'In fact, I *insist* upon you staying.'

'Sure I'll stay, ma'am,' Tiny concurred, having been compelled to halt by the girl blocking his way. 'Happen that's what *you* want.'

'It is, sir, it is!' Charlotte confirmed, so quickly and fervently that Nolly was worried in case she might be overacting. Swinging her gaze to him, she continued, 'It's Terry, Uncle Ossie – !'

'Charlotte's elder brother and, of course, my nephew, sir,' the Bostonian interrupted. 'A good, church going and intelligent young man, although I'd be the first to admit he's inclined to be a trifle impetuous on occasion.'

'He certainly has been *this* time!' Charlotte admitted vehemently, hiding her amusement over hearing her 'brother' described as 'good' and 'church going'. Looking alarmed, she went to slump rather than sit in the chair vacated by the bearded giant, but took care that her cloak did not open to spoil the effect by exhibiting the rest of her attire. 'Yet he *is* right about that window, even though he shouldn't have let himself be goaded into making that foolish bet – !'

'And what, may I ask, is the nature of this foolish and ill advised wager, my dear?' Nolly requested, after the girl had allowed the words to trail to an end as if overcome by the enormity of what had happened. He saw with satisfaction, that Tiny's face was registering a growing concern.

Continuing to act with a skill which might have earned her a high reputation in the theatre if she had not embraced a life of crime, Charlotte told the story which Nolly had outlined for her. She explained that her 'brother' was employed by Wells Fargo & Company. On being sent to Mulrooney as an assistant agent, he had become perturbed by the discovery of what he considered to be a serious flaw in the local office's security arrangements. While the rest of the building was adequately defended against unauthorised entry, a small window opening on the alley at the northern end offered a possible means of access, despite being equipped with strong iron bars. On pointing out to his superior that the bars were not as firmly fixed as those on the other windows, he had been informed – as the alley was far too narrow to allow horses to be hitched to them as an aid to ripping them from their fittings – that they were secure enough.

'And,' the girl concluded indignantly, 'even though Brother Terry reminded him that somebody called Mark Counter had done something similar in another town, that stupid man just laughed when he suggested an exceptionally strong man might be able to pull them out with his bare hands.'

'Egad, yes! I too have heard of Mr Counter performing such a feat,' Nolly claimed truthfully, the exploit having been the source of his inspiration for what he had in mind.[1] 'And, although I have not seen the aforesaid window, I don't doubt my nephew is correct in his summation.'

'Neither would *anybody* who knows him!' Charlotte asserted. 'But you *know* what he is like when he's aroused. He bet the agent a thousand dollars that he can not only get inside, but carry away the safe – Well, not him personally, but somebody he had found who was strong enough to do it.'

'A *thousand* dollars,' Nolly gasped. 'Good heavens, my dear. Munificent as your parents are, I was not aware that he is in possession of such a considerable sum.'

'That's just the trouble!' Charlotte wailed. 'He *isn't*. So he won't be able to pay when he loses!'

'*When?*' Nolly repeated. 'But I thought it was your assertion that he could command the services of a man with sufficiently Herculean thews to ensure he won?'

'He had,' Charlotte explained. 'But the man he had in

[1] When and how Mark Counter performed the feat in question is told in: *Part One, 'Better Than Calamity', THE WILDCATS.* J.T.E.

mind met with an accident and won't be able to do it for him.'

'By now, sir,' Nolly remarked, looking straight at Tiny for the first time since the conversation had commenced. 'You are, no doubt, commencing to suspect that you are about to be subjected to a request for the necessary funds with which the losses of a non-existent brother can be paid?'

'Well, no – !' the bearded giant began, although such a thought had occurred to him.

'I assure you such is far from being the case, my good sir,' Nolly interrupted, reaching inside the red velvet smoking jacket he had donned to convey the impression that he had no intention of leaving the room. Taking out his wallet, he showed it was well supplied with money. 'I have here more than a sufficiency to pay off my nephew's debt of honour, ill-advised though acquiring it may have been, and will not hesitate to do so as he has had the misfortune to be unable to justify his confidence. However, I would much prefer that he should win and not, I hasten to ask you to believe, merely for crass monetary gain. If my nephew says there is a flaw in the arrangements for protecting the property of those who entrust it to his office's care, then sir, a flaw *must* exist and needs to be eradicated. The problem is, how would it be possible to vindicate him?'

'If only the man Brother Terry was relying upon hadn't hurt himself,' Charlotte put in. 'I wish we could find *somebody* strong enough to replace him.'

'I'm pretty strong, ma'am,' Tiny pointed out.

'Egad yes, so you are!' Nolly ejaculated, acting as if he had overlooked the point until it was brought to his attention. 'And, from what I saw you do outside Henry's Saloon, you possess the muscular prowess needed to pluck the bars out – But we can't impose upon your good nature to such an extent, sir.'

'Aw shucks!' Tiny protested, as the girl directed a look which appeared to be filled with pleading at him. 'It'd be a right poor sort of world iffen we couldn't help one another out. Happen the agent won't be too riled should I be able to haul them bars out, I'll be happy to give it a whirl.'

'He *won't* be,' Charlotte declared reassuringly. 'In fact, he told Brother Terry that he'll have them replaced out of his own pocket if he loses the bet.'

'That's fine then,' the bearded giant said. 'I'll give her a whirl in the morning.'

'It has to be tonight!' the girl replied, too quickly for Nolly's liking.

'Tonight?' Tiny repeated.

'A most sound move, if one thinks about it, sir,' the Bostonian remarked. 'After all, Wells Fargo would hardly wish it to become known that they had put the goods entrusted to their care into jeopardy. Nobody will be present to see the experiment take place tonight.'

'Will the agent be there?' Tiny asked.

'No,' Charlotte replied. Nolly had envisaged the possibility of the question and, in addition to supplying an answer, had produced a reason for the other members of the gang to be present. 'But he's arranged for some of his men to be witnesses.'

'I hope that will be satisfactory, sir?' Nolly asked and knew that the success or failure of his efforts was hanging in the balance.

CHAPTER TWELVE

HE WON'T BE TROUBLING US

Having been established in the vicinity of the railroad depot, for the convenience of those who were travelling by train or its own stagecoaches, the office of Wells Fargo & Company was in an area devoted to various kinds of business premises rather than places of entertainment. Although there were sounds of celebrations elsewhere, despite the time being close to midnight, the Wells Fargo office and its immediate surroundings were almost devoid of human life when Tiny Crumble arrived with Charlotte Solikin and Oswald Nolly. In fact, the only person to be seen was a tall, ruggedly handsome and well built young man standing by the rear door of the office building. He was wearing a brown derby hat, a matching three-piece suit of the latest Eastern fashion, a dark blue woollen turtle-necked sweater and Hersome gaiter boots.

'Mr Crumble has offered to help you win your bet, Brother Terry!' the girl announced, running ahead of the two men as if so delighted she could not wait to deliver the news. 'Isn't that *kind* of him?'

'Kind's not the word for it,' Terrence Rushton answered, his accent indicating that he came from the same part of Boston as Charlotte. However, he was a far less accomplished actor than her and something of the big city dweller's derision for those he considered to be dull witted hayseeds – particularly when circumstances made it appear the classification was correct – was evident in his tone. 'No, I wouldn't say ki – !'

'Where are Mr Miscowitz and the other gentlemen, *nephew*?' Nolly interrupted curtly, hoping that the bearded giant had not detected and taken offence at his 'maternal kinsman's' attitude.

In spite of his first misgivings, Tiny had fallen into the trap prepared for him by the Bostonian and the girl. This was less a criticism of his intelligence than a tribute to their histrionic abilities. Charlotte had spent most of her life playing upon the sympathies of men and had succeeded with some who were far more worldly and less susceptible than him. Nor could Nolly's contribution be overlooked. In fact, it had been a major factor. He had already gained the bearded giant's confidence before she put in an appearance and he continued to play upon the other's emotions with consummate skill.

While the girl had gone to her room and sent Rushton – who was waiting impatiently – to inform the rest of the gang that the plan could go ahead, Nolly had contrived to examine the furs without arousing Tiny's suspicion over his claim to be a dealer. He had quoted a price which, after some friendly haggling, had proved most acceptable to the bearded giant. Such had been his 'generosity' that Tiny had no longer felt the slightest concern over the task which lay ahead, but was convinced that – as Nolly approved of the attempt being made – everything must be all right.

The pleasant events of the day had also played their part in helping to render the bearded giant more vulnerable than might otherwise have been the case. Drinking beer always tended to increase his normal amiability and willingness to help others. What was more, the friendly treatment he had received earlier had made him less inclined to question motives than if he had been subjected to the kind of abuse which had ruined visits to other towns. Taken with what he had believed to be the success of his self-imposed mission and filled with thoughts of the approbation which would be forthcoming when he returned home to tell of the lucrative new market he had discovered, he was in a far from critical mood.

'Miskie's gone over to make sure the Pink – ' Rushton began. Then, drawing the correct conclusion from the warning hiss and glance at Tiny delivered by his 'sister', he hurriedly revised the far from discreet comment he had been on the point of making. 'He's down the street with 'Digger and Gil.'

'Then you'd better go and have the buckboard fetched,' Nolly ordered, having watched carefully for and been relieved when he did not see anything to lead him to assume their intended dupe's suspicions had been aroused. He was however disinclined to chance his tactless accomplice making an error which could bring this about. He also had to know whether another part of his scheme had been carried out before he continued with their plan. 'Come, Mr Crumble, sir. Let me show you the window.'

'Why sure, Mr Nolly,' Tiny assented, speaking in his usual gently drawling fashion. Although he considered 'Brother Terry' was a far less likeable person than 'Miss Charlotte', or the stocky Easterner, he decided that he could not hold it against them and he failed to draw any other conclusions. 'The sooner we get at it, the sooner we'll be through and go have those beers I promised you.'

'I can think of no more equitable arrangement, my good sir,' Nolly asserted, sounding as though he believed the promised beer would be forthcoming and he was looking forward to drinking it.

'Here they come now, Uncle Ossie,' the girl remarked, as three men appeared at the other end of the alley.

Halting the trio, Rushton delivered Nolly's message and Arnold Kilburn set off to collect the vehicle. Leaving Rushton and Gilbert Tamar looking along the street, the man who had killed Reg Wall ambled forward. The fourth member of the gang was dressed in the same general fashion as Rushton, about the same age and build as Kilburn and, if anything, more brutal featured than Miscowitz.

'Is everything all right?' Nolly asked in Polish, having no more faith in the burly man's tact than he had where Rushton was concerned.

'It was even easier than we counted on,' Miscowitz answered, also employing his native tongue. 'They must have decided Hosper wouldn't be coming around to check on them tonight. Gil followed Garvey down to Lily Gouch's place just after we got here and said he looked like he was going to stay awhile.'

'So only Bilson was over there?' Nolly assessed, glancing at an unlit and apparently deserted building at the other side of the street. 'Did you have any trouble getting to him?'

'None. I just gave that trick knock they've been using and he opened up straight away,' the Pole replied and leered as he tapped his right hip pocket. 'He won't be bothering us.'

'I've never seen such a man as Uncle Ossie when it comes to knowing foreign lauguages, Mr Crumble,' Charlotte remarked in a conspiratorial tone, having seen a puzzled expression come to the bearded giant's face and seeking to allay any suspicions aroused by hearing Nolly addressing Miscowitz in such a fashion. 'And, as so much of his business back home is done with people who don't speak a great deal of English, he finds it useful to practice at every opportunity.'

'I reckon it would be,' Tiny replied, accepting the explanation. 'I don't speak nothing 'cept English myself.'

'Neither do I,' Charlotte admitted. 'Shall we look at the window?'

'Is he hurt badly?' Nolly inquired, noticing with approval that the girl was distracting the bearded giant and continuing to speak Polish.

'Bad enough,' Miscowitz answered, just a trifle defiantly.

'Is he *dead*?' Nolly demanded, having no illusions where the brutal nature of the burly man was concerned.

'He wound up that way,' Miscowitz admitted, then continued in exculpation. 'I never thought a god-damned Pink-Eye would have such a soft head.'

'Go and tell Rushton to keep watch on the back,' Nolly ordered, hiding his irritation with an effort. His instructions had been that the men who had the office under surveillance were to be prevented from being able to raise the alarm. Although he would have preferred it to be done in a less lethal fashion, he knew the Pole too well to be surprised that there had been a killing. Despite suspecting it had been done deliberately and without any justifiable reason, he realised nothing would be gained by complaining. 'You and Gil stay down there in case Garvey comes back before we're through.'

'He'll soon wish he hadn't if he does!' Miscowitz threatened, once again fingering the pocket in which he was carrying the sap he had used both to end the pickpocket's life earlier in the day, and reduce the watcher's skull to a bloody, brain-oozing pulp. Then he nodded to where Charlotte was pointing out the small window to the bearded giant. 'Let's hope he's worth all the god-damned waiting around *we've* been doing.'

'I'll bet my share of the loot he is,' Nolly stated, knowing the sullen comment stemmed mainly from his 'waiting' having been done in the Fair Lady Saloon while the rest of the gang had been compelled to remain in less salubrious surroundings except when paying the brief visits to learn how he was progressing. 'Do you want to take me?'

'Not me!' Miscowitz replied vehemently. 'One thing I've learned is *never* to take any bets against *you*.'

'Go back and keep watch for Garvey then,' the Bostonian commanded. 'We'll soon know one way or the other.'

'Well, Mr Crumble,' Charlotte was saying, as the Pole went by and Nolly joined her. 'Do you think you can pull out the bars?'

'I dunno until I've tried, ma'am,' Tiny admitted. 'But I'll surely do the best I can for you.'

'I must confess that I am looking forward with great interest to seeing you make the – I have no doubt – completely successful attempt, sir,' Nolly declared and there was a genuine note of sincerity in his voice.

When carrying out a reconnaissance on his arrival in Mulrooney, the Bostonian had concluded that the small window offered the easiest – in fact, under the circumstances, the only – point of entry to the otherwise impregnable building. Not that gaining admittance even there would be a sinecure. The two stout iron bars were set in a frame of the same metal which was attached to the surrounding wood of the wall by sturdy nuts and bolts. The heads of the latter were countersunk in such a fashion that they could not be unfastened from the outside. However, if the bars could be removed, the window gave access to a small storeroom which an investigation had established was never fastened in any way.

The major problem with which Nolly had found himself faced was how to remove the bars in the quickest possible time. Even on Independence Day, the marshal's deputies would be making the rounds and, if they had been informed of what the safe contained, they would supplement the efforts of the watchers across the street by making regular visits.

When Nolly had suggested pulling out the bars, Miscowitz – who usually provided whatever muscle power and brute strength was required – had stated it would not be possible. Because of the window's small size, there was room for only one man to pull and there was no way in the narrow alley by which horses could provide the means of traction. Until the Bostonian had seen Mark Counter and the bearded giant lifting the wagon, he had reconciled himself to what he had known would be a lengthy session of cutting with a hacksaw. Recollecting the earlier feat performed by the blond giant, he had decided to try and trick the big hunter into helping them, thus reducing the period of waiting. Having succeeded in obtaining Tiny's help and having been informed that the precautionary measure of removing the only watcher who was on duty had been accomplished, he wanted no further delay before discovering whether his confidence would be justified.

'Aren't those gents coming with your nephew to watch me?' Tiny inquired, glancing to where Rushton was returning.

'No,' Nolly replied. 'Mr Miscowitz was just telling me that the agent said they should stand lookout and prevent anybody discovering what we are doing. It would do his company no good should the public become cognisant with the danger posed by the flimsy protection of this window.'

'I reckon it wouldn't at that,' the bearded giant conceded. 'Well, let's give her a whirl.'

Stepping forward, Tiny raised his hands to shoulder height and grasped the bars. While Miscowitz had pointed out with justification that they were too high for him to be able to exert his full strength against them, their position was ideal where the taller hunter was concerned. Giving a tentative tug, he instinctively assessed what he learned from it. He could not have explained the faculty in words, but he possessed an intuitive flair for calculating the effects of the stresses and strains he created. The slight movement he had felt suggested that his task was not as impossible as it might appear.

After darting a confident grin at the watching couple and receiving a smile of encouragement from the girl, Tiny placed his right foot against the wall. Oblivious of its true purpose, he began to devote every ounce of his strength to the task he had been tricked into carrying out. While his tremendously powerful arms, shoulders and back supplied the force to pull out the bars, his equally puissant gluteus, thigh and calf muscles were applying pressure in the other direction.

At first, there was nothing other than a muted creaking sound. It increased in volume. Then, with a sharp splintering crackle as the wood of the wall gave way under the enormous strain being inflicted upon it, the bolts tore free and the entire frame separated from its surroundings. This was followed by a clatter and the crash of glass breaking as, deprived of support, the window fell into the building.

'He did it!' Charlotte gasped, watching the bearded giant stagger backwards with the frame and bars in his hands.

'I never doubted that he would, my dear,' Nolly replied, contriving to sound as if he was speaking the truth. Then he glanced along the alley and his voice took on an angry intonation as he reverted to speaking Polish. 'Make sure that nobody's heard us, damn you!'

'It's all right, nobody has!' Miscowitz called after a moment, having turned from where he had been watching what was happening instead of carrying out the duty to which he was assigned. He scanned the street in both directions. 'Shall I – ?'

'You stay there and keep watch!' Nolly commanded and, swinging around, began to speak English again in an amiable tone. 'Congratulations, my good sir. Egad, may I say you have fully justified all my expectations.'

'I said I'd give her a whirl,' Tiny pointed out, breathing heavily and setting down his burden. 'Only I don't reckon I'm small enough to get through the window.'

'Have no fear, sir,' Nolly answered, waving a hand towards Charlotte. 'That contingency has been contemplated.'

While the conversation had been taking place, the girl had slipped off her cloak. In doing so, she revealed why she had taken so much care to prevent it opening in her 'uncle's' room. Instead of the decorous attire she had worn earlier, she now had on a skin-tight black bodice with an extreme *décolletée* that revealed more than it concealed, and matching tights.

Much to her amusement as she was removing her shoes, Charlotte heard Tiny let out a startled exclamation. Looking over her shoulder, she sensed that he was blushing as he turned hurriedly away. Deciding against embarrassing him further by asking him to help her, she went to the wall. While climbing through the window, with Nolly's assistance, she realised that she alone of the gang could have obtained entrance in such a fashion. Once inside, she took the bull's eye lantern which the Bostonian had brought from the hotel. Opening its front, she illuminated her way across the store-room and into the main office.

'Ah, here comes Mr Kilburn with the buckboard, sir,' Nolly remarked, after the girl had disappeared into the building. 'Shall we join him?'

'Why sure,' Tiny replied, then threw a worried look at the ruined window. 'Will it be all right for me to come, seeing's how Miss Charlotte's undress – the way she is?'

'Your concern does you credit, sir,' Nolly declared. 'However, it is uncalled for. Her leotard – named, as you undoubtedly know, after the great French aerialist of that cognomen – is quite acceptable attire for a young lady when her "uncle" and "brother" are present.'

Reassured, although he had no idea what an 'aerialist' might be, Tiny waited until the Bostonian had gathered up the girl's attire and accompanied him to the rear of the building. Following the lead given by Nolly, Rushton thanked the bearded giant for having made her entrance to the building possible and Kilburn added his congratulations. By the time this was done, the rear door opened and Charlotte emerged. Skilled at picking locks, she had had no need to do so. A key hung on a hook alongside the door. Using it in the lock and drawing the two bolts, she was able to allow the men to enter.

'Do you require any help with the safe, sir?' Nolly inquired.

'I reckon I can manage it,' Tiny answered.

Crossing to the steel depository, the bearded giant enfolded it in his arms. Such was his strength that, despite all the calls made upon it by ripping away the bars, he contrived to lift and carry it from the office. Helped by the other three men, he set it down on the bed of the buckboard which Kilburn had hired for that purpose and left nearby to be collected when needed.

'By gad, sir,' Nolly boomed, taking a small silver flask from his jacket's inside pocket. 'After what you have done for my nephew, I must insist that you have a drink.'

'I reckon I could use it,' Tiny admitted.

While drinking, the bearded giant thought the liquid had a bitter taste. Returning the flask, he was about to ask when the safe was to be returned. Then a wave of dizziness assailed him. His legs buckled and he measured his length on the ground.

'Is he dead?' Charlotte asked, feeling sorry for their victim in spite of her generally hard boiled nature.

'Of course not,' Nolly replied, kneeling and taking a key from Tiny's pocket. 'Here, 'Digger. Go along to the Fair Lady Saloon. This will let you into an empty room at the back where he's supposed to be sleeping. Bring away his rifle and anything else belonging to him. We'll not be going speedily, so you will easily catch up with us en route to the cabin.'

'Sure, Ossie,' Kilburn assented.

'Pass me that rope,' Nolly told Rushton. 'After I've bound him securely, help me load him on the buckboard and we will be on our way.'

'Why not leave him here?' the younger man asked.

'Because I don't want him found,' Nolly replied. 'His disappearance will ensure that the minions of law and order, whether from the marshal's office or those employed by Mr Pinkerton, blame him for what has taken place.'

'He'll tell them different when they get him,' Rushton warned. 'Or are you going to leave him dead at the cabin?'

'There will be no need for us to do so,' Nolly stated with complete assurance. 'After what has happened to their associate, the minions of Mr Pinkerton will be all too willing to do it for us.'

CHAPTER THIRTEEN

YOU KNEW WHO AND WHAT I AM

'Mark! Open up, it's Kail Beauregard!'

The pounding on the door woke him up and, as he was not alone in bed, Mark Counter found the announcement rather disturbing. Yet, although she had looked and behaved like a properly raised and respectable young lady downstairs in the bar-room, his naked and beautiful blonde companion showed remarkable restraint. In fact, she betrayed little of the alarm which such an event as the marshal's arrival might have been expected to arouse in a person of her apparent background.

'Is it *you* he's after?' Mark inquired quietly, rolling from the bed and picking up his Levis trousers.

'I really don't see how it could be,' the girl replied, showing neither surprise nor annoyance over the question. 'Waco told you how I looked when we met at the railroad depot, so I wasn't recognised between there and the hotel.'

'How about here?'

'I could have been. But that wouldn't explain why Kail would come *here* looking for me. Nobody followed me when I left – or came back.'

'Anyway,' the blond giant drawled, having donned the trousers, walking across the room, 'even if Kail had found out you were here, he'd have left it until morning before coming after you.'

Waiting until the blonde had drawn the covers over her head, although he was equally certain her true identity had not been exposed, Mark opened the door. He found that Marshal Kail Beauregard was not alone. Standing in the passage, which was illuminated by a couple of lamps suspended from the ceiling, were a deputy, the agent of Wells Fargo & Company – who was clearly not long from his bed and was worried over something – and two more men.

The latter pair wore derby hats, town suits and footwear, but had Western-style gunbelts carrying revolvers strapped around their waists. The taller and heavier had an air of swaggering self importance which suggested he considered himself to be a person of great consequence. Mark recognised him as Morgan Hosper, a senior operative of the Pinkerton National Detective Agency and he noticed that his normally arrogant features were suffused by anger. Slightly shorter, not so expensively dressed, but equally brawny, the other man had the surly, hangdog look of one who realises he has fallen badly from grace in some respect.

'Howdy, Kail, gents,' the blond giant greeted, guessing the second man was also a Pinkerton operative. 'What's wrong?'

'Sorry to wake you, *amigo*,' Beauregard apologised. 'But have you-all any idea where Tiny Crumble might be?'

'Downstairs, sleeping in the empty room at the back, as far as I know,' Mark replied, glancing along the passage and discovering that the other three members of the floating outfit had also been disturbed. They were coming, dressed in the same fashion as himself, from the rooms they were respectively occupying. 'He allowed he was tired early on and turned in.'

'He's not there *now*!' Hosper growled.

'Could be the noise was too much for him to sleep in there,' Mark suggested, making it plain the words were directed to the marshal rather than the speaker. 'So he's likely gone to find some place a mite quieter.'

'And maybe he never aimed to sleep there at all,' hinted the man at Hosper's side, in a sullen New England accent, his attitude redolent of one who had a guilty conscience or had been found wanting.

'How about telling me what's going on, Kail?' Mark requested.

'Somebody broke into the Wells Fargo office – !' Beauregard began.

'Broke *into*!' the New Englander interrupted bitterly, his voice rising. 'God-damn it, the son-of-a-bitch left Lennie Bilson with his head beat to a pulp, ripped the "something" bars out of the "mother-something" wall and – !'

'I'll thank you to lower your voice and clean up your

language!'[1] Freddie Woods commanded, as she strode along the passage fastening the robe she had donned before – although none of the men had noticed – following Dusty Fog from her bedroom.

'Shut your mouth, Garvey!' Hosper snarled and, making a visible effort, he managed to put a less truculent timbre to his normally harsh voice as he turned to the beautiful Englishwoman. 'I'm sorry to have disturbed you, Miss Woods, but it's important.'

'I don't doubt *that*,' Freddie conceded. Despite her usually immaculate hair and facial make-up being dishevelled and her informal attire notwithstanding, she still presented a commanding appearance. Pointing to a door at the other side of the passage, she went on in a tone which suggested she would brook no refusal, 'But I *suggest* that any further discussion takes place in my sitting-room so it won't disturb any of my other guests.'

'There's no need for any *discussion* – ma'am!' Hosper protested, as the other men – with the exception of Garvey – started to walk in the direction indicated by the woman. 'All we want to know is where to find that big – jasper.'

'We'll do the talking in here!' Beauregard stated, rather than suggested, opening the door. 'And thanks for the offer, Miss Woods.'

'Are *you* sure that it was Tiny who broke into the office, Kail?' Mark asked, after the party had assembled in the sitting-room and the lamp on the table had been lit.

'There aren't too many other men around who'd be strong enough to have done it,' the marshal replied, noticing how three distinct groups had been formed. The Texans stood together, as did the two operatives. Showing the kind of tact he had come to expect from her, Freddie was with the town dwellers who had gathered around him. 'Not the way everything had been done, anyhow. On top of which, he's gone. Miss Woods's swamper let us in and showed us where he should have been bedded down. He wasn't there and neither was his pack and rifle.'

'That doesn't prove he did it,' Dusty pointed out.

'Like the marshal said,' Hosper growled, noticing how – when seen stripped to the waist – the small Texan's muscular

[1] See the second paragraph of the Author's Note on Page 7. J.T.E.

development was far greater than he had imagined. 'There aren't too many other men around who could have torn the bars out of the window.'

'Would that be the little window in the alley at the north end of the office, Kail?' Waco put in.

'It was,' Beauregard replied.

'And there hadn't been a fu – horse used to do it!' Garvey supplemented, breaking off the intended obscenity as he saw the hostility with which everybody else was looking at him. He was smarting under the knowledge that his neglect of duty had allowed the robbery to be committed and did not want the added complication of a complaint made to his superiors by a person as important as the Englishwoman. 'So it *must've* been him.'

'Whoever got in'd've had to be a whole heap smaller than Tiny,' Waco objected. 'Even with the bars gone, that old window wouldn't've been anywheres big enough for a feller his size to climb through.'

'I'm not gainsaying that,' Beauregard answered, having heard from Dusty about the blond youngster's flair for deductive reasoning and concluding he was seeing an example of it.[2] 'But the robbery wasn't a one-man chore.'

'Likely,' Waco assented. 'And it wasn't fixed up today, neither.'

'What's that mean?' Hosper asked, scowling.

'Whoever did it had to've been around for long enough to do some scouting,' the youngster explained, showing not the slightest concern over the baleful looks he was receiving from Hosper and Garvey. 'Which Tiny only came into town today.'

'Or so *he* said!' Hosper sniffed disdainfully.

'A *hombre* his size would be hard to hide out,' Waco countered.

'It could be done, though,' Beauregard commented, although he was inclined to concur with the youngster's summation. 'Or it could have been timed so's he'd get here the day they needed him. Did he do much talking to anybody while he was with you fellers?'

[2] New readers can find information regarding books giving examples of Waco's abilities in the field of deductive reasoning in, *APPENDIX FOUR* J.T.E.

'Not that I noticed,' the blond giant replied, the question having been directed at him. 'At least, he didn't spend much time away from us or seem to be looking for somebody.'

'You said the safe had been carried away, Kail,' Dusty remarked. 'There'd have to be something real special in it for them to take so much trouble.'

'There *was* something special in it,' the Wells Fargo agent affirmed coldly, throwing a far from amiable look at Hosper. 'A collection of jewellery worth over a hundred and fifty thousand dollars. It's been there since the end of last month, but *nobody* got around to telling *me* what it was or I'd let you know, as we arranged, and could have put some men on guard at the office.'

'It was bought back East by a rich mine owner up in Virginia City and we'd been hired to bring it here for him to collect,' the senior operative explained, as several pairs of eyes swung in an accusatory manner at him. 'Hell, having to come all the way down from Montana, he couldn't say to a day just when he'd arrive. We didn't want word getting around, so we never said what was in the packet when we brought it to you.'

'It makes me feel *real* good to know how much I'm trusted!' the agent snorted.

'And me!' Beauregard seconded grimly.

'We've been keeping a watch of our own over the office every night,' Hosper answered, directing a vicious scowl at Garvey.

'There's some's might say you wasn't watching close enough tonight,' the Ysabel Kid drawled sardonically, having a typical Southerner's antipathy where members of the Pinkerton National Detective Agency was concerned. 'Which you-all don't look to go keeping your secrets any too good, neither. 'Cause somebody sure's sin's for sale in Cowtown[3] found this one out.'

'What's that mean?' Garvey challenged, his conscience – or rather his concern for the future – causing him to resent reminders about his shortcomings.

'Shut your god-damned mouth!' Hosper snarled furiously. After his companion had lapsed into a sulky silence, he went

[3] 'Cowtown' : a colloquial name for Fort Worth, Tarrant County, Texas. J.T.E.

on in a slightly less hostile fashion, 'I don't suppose the big feller said anything that'd maybe help us to find him, did he, Mr Counter?'

The knowledge that he too was far from blameless, as he had left his subordinates without supervision to enjoy the company of a compliant woman he had met at the Railroad House Hotel, had put the savage note in the operative's voice when he was addressing Garvey. However, he was aware that his own future in the organisation was in jeopardy and had swallowed his resentment over the Kid's mocking comment in order to get assistance from the blond giant.

'Not a thing,' Mark replied. 'He allowed it was the first time he'd been here and he didn't know anybody in town – Which I don't reckon he'd've been likely to tell me where he was figuring on hiding after he'd helped rob the Wells Fargo office.'

'So *you* reckon he did it, huh?' Hosper asked hopefully.

'No, *you* reckon he did,' the blond giant corrected. 'Back home to Texas, we reckon a man's innocent until he's been proven guilty.'

'We'll soon enough prove *that* when we get him!' Hosper declared and Garvey nodded in equally vehement agreement.

'If you'll wait until we're dressed, Kail,' Dusty drawled, turning his gaze from the two operatives. 'We'll come and lend you a hand to look around.'

'I'll be right pleased to have you-all,' Beauregard assented, accepting that the members of the floating outfit possessed a more extensive knowledge of the town than he had yet acquired and considering their assistance might prove invaluable. 'With that safe along, they won't have travelled far and they're likely to be holed up someplace.' His voice became less friendly as he continued, 'You two can come with me, *Mr* Hosper.'

'We could work separately – !' the senior operative began.

'Working *separately*, as you call it, is what's got this damned business going in the first place,' Beauregard interrupted coldly. 'If you'd told us what was in the safe, it could have been guarded properly. Instead, you kept quiet and hid around ready to grab the glory happen somebody did learn and tried to steal it. So from now on, you work with me – and I aim to bring in whoever did it alive, if I can.'

'I agree wholeheartedly!' Freddie went on, deducing from Hosper's scowl that at least part of his reason for secrecy had been exposed. 'And I hope Marshal Beauregard can catch them for you. But, whether he does or not, *I'll* be writing to Mr Pinkerton and will tell him exactly what happened and that I'll appreciate better co-operation with the marshal's office in the future.'

* * * * *

'Did *you* know what was in the safe at the Wells Fargo office?' Mark Counter asked, having turned up the light of the lamp on the bedside table on his return from the discussion in the sitting room.

That the blond giant should have asked such a question of the beautiful young woman with whom he had been sleeping was no more surprising than his earlier inquiry over whether she was the cause of Marshal Kail Beauregard's visit. Although she was a well known outlaw, he and Belle Starr had been on intimate terms for some time.[4]

'Only since just after I left Waco this afternoon,' the girl replied, having arrived in Mulrooney so well disguised – including special make-up and a false nose – that the youngster had not known she was the 'schoolteacher' from the railroad depot until she told him in the bar-room. Sitting up and showing no resentment over the question in spite of guessing what had caused it, she went on, 'That wasn't what brought me here. I was passing and thought I'd drop by to say, "Howdy, you-all" before *you* headed back to Texas.'

'Lady,' Mark drawled, leaning across the bed to deliver a kiss. 'I can't think of when it's been said nicer.'

'Why thank you 'most to death, kind sir,' Belle answered, throwing back the covers as the blond giant started to remove his trousers. However, when he picked up his union suit instead of joining her, she pouted and went on, 'Blast those jewels. Why couldn't they be stolen some other night?'

'You knew they were going to be stolen?' Mark asked, pausing as he was drawing up the long-legged underpants

[4] For the benefit of new readers, see *Footnote 8, APPENDIX TWO.* J.T.E.

which were attached to the undershirt to form a complete garment.

'I did,' the blonde confessed, just a trifle defiantly.

'And reckoned you'd best have an alibi in case it happened?' Mark challenged.

'God damn you, Mark Counter!' Belle yelped, sitting up again. 'You knew who and what I am before you took me into your bed, so – !'

'You're so quick to temper, gal, I often wonder why I chance it,' the blond giant said with a grin, laying a massive right hand on the girl's face and shoving her gently if firmly down. 'So you knew the jewels were going to be wide-looped tonight – ?'

'The hell I did, you big son-of-a-loving-bitch!' Belle protested. 'I just knew somebody was going to make a stab at it.'

'That stab went right home to the Green River,[5] gal,' Mark declared. 'How'd you get to know – and, so help me, should you get riled again, next time I bed a gal, it'll be Calamity Jane.'[6]

'Hot damn if I'd want even you to do *that*!' Belle chuckled, lying back on the bed. 'I'll admit I knew they were going to be stolen, but not tonight. In fact, from what I read, I didn't think they would be.'

'How did you-all find out what was going to happen?' Mark wanted to know. 'Unless it's something you can't tell me in case it gets somebody you know in waters over the willows and with the river still rising.'

'It isn't,' Belle admitted, being acquainted with the Texan's term for one of the most dangerous situations encountered during a trail drive. Explaining how she had acquired her information while the blond giant continued to don his clothes, she concluded, 'But I still don't see why *you* have to go and help Kail Beauregard look for them!'

[5] A colloquialism meaning to kill. First manufactured in 1834 at Greenfield, Massachusetts – on the banks of the Green River – a very popular type of knife had the maker's name, 'J. Russell & Co./Green River Works', inscribed along the blade just below the guard of the hilt. Any knife driven into a human adversary 'up to the Green River' was likely to prove fatal whether the inscription was there or not. J.T.E.

[6] For the benefit of new readers: information regarding various meetings between Mark Counter and Miss Martha 'Calamity Jane' Canary are given in; *Footnote 7, APPENDIX TWO*. J.T.E.

'It's this way, honey,' Mark explained. 'There are a couple of Pink-Eyes involved and they're trying to lay the blame on a feller we both know.'

'Tiny Crumble?' Belle asked.

'Tiny Crumble,' Mark agreed, wondering if he might have been wrong in assuming the bearded giant was innocent.

'You-all like him, don't you?' the blonde said, more as a statement than a question, swinging her legs from the bed and standing to display her naked, magnificently contoured body unashamedly.

'I like him,' Mark confirmed, pulling on his shirt.

'Well he's not in it,' Belle declared. 'At least, not intentionally. The jasper who made the plan needed somebody to help him get into the office and, from what I saw of Tiny, he'd be the kind who would.'

'He's not stupid!' Mark objected.

'No,' the blonde acceded. 'But, as soon as I saw the width of that alley, I knew they couldn't be using a horse. Then I remembered what happened when you met Calam and Madam Bulldog in Tennyson and got to wondering if *you* could haul the bars out like you did in the jail down there. When I met Tiny, I knew there were two of you in town who could do it – And don't get riled. I *know* the only way he would was if somebody slickered him into it. A nice feller like him, it would be easy to do.'

'You're not wrong about that, honey,' Mark conceded. 'He's such a honest and trusting cuss himself, I reckon it wouldn't be too hard to do.'

'It wouldn't,' Belle confirmed, speaking with the voice of practical experience. 'Anyways, you can maybe find them if you go out to the Grenley place, should you know where that is.'

'It's about three miles west of town,' the blond giant said quietly, knowing the blonde had supplied the information out of the goodness of her heart and because of her genuine love for him. 'Have you any notion how many of them will be there?'

'Five men and a girl, I'd say,' Belle supplied. 'Likely they'll all be together. I don't reckon any of them would trust the others out of their sight with the safe.'

'Just five men and a gal, huh?' Mark drawled, then

scooped the blonde into his arms. '*Gracias, querida!*'

'I liked Tiny too,' Belle pointed out, after they had kissed. 'Besides, I don't want you to have to spend too long looking for him. I have to leave on the noon train.'

'I'll certain sure keep *that* in mind, honey-child,' the blond giant promised, lifting the girl as if she weighed no more than a newly born baby and dropping her on the bed. 'You-all just lie there like that until I get back and, hot damn, I'll say, "Why thank you, ma'am" the best way I know how.'

'Like hell I'll just lie here a-waiting!' Belle purred, wriggling her voluptuous body in provocative anticipation in a way she would never show to another man. 'I'm going to get back under these warm and snug old covers again so I'll be all warm and welcome for you when you come.'

'Now that's what I like,' Mark drawled, concluding his dressing by strapping on his gunbelt and lashing the pigging thongs to his thighs. 'A real thoughtful kind of loving gal.'

'Damned if there are times I don't think you deserve me!' Belle sniffed.

'So do I, not that I'd tell you,' Mark replied, crossing to the left side wall and banging on it. When a feminine voice with a pronounced Cockney accent asked what he wanted, he continued, 'Tell Waco to pass the word to Lon that the three of us'll be needing moccasins, Babsy.'

'All right, love,' responded Freddie's buxom, vivacious little maid-travelling companion. 'What about Cap'n Dusty?'

'He won't be needing them,' the blond giant assessed. 'This's work for us hired hands.'

CHAPTER FOURTEEN

WHO WANTS THINGS *TOO* EASY?

'Belle called it right, *amigo*,' the Ysabel Kid stated, after he had carried out a reconnaisance of the homestead which had already become ramshackled and dilapidated before the departure of the Grenley family. He strolled through the semi-darkness to where Mark Counter and Waco were waiting with their horses and his big white stallion. 'They're there all right – And Tiny's with them.'

As the blond giant had requested, when he and the other members of the OD Connected's floating outfit had returned to the sitting-room, only Dusty Fog was wearing boots. The small Texan had demonstrated that he too possessed deductive ability by suggesting, without needing to consult with Mark, that he went with Marshal Kail Beauregard's party while his *amigos* conducted an independent search. He had drawn his conclusion because he knew with whom the big blond was spending the night and he guessed that Belle Starr had supplied information which could prove embarrassing for her if anybody else learned she had supplied it.

Despite having glanced at the trio's footwear, the marshal had not commented upon its specialised nature. Nor, for all his earlier insistence that the Pinkerton operatives remained with him, had he shown any hesitation in concurring with Dusty's suggestions about the way in which the investigation should be conducted.

Collecting their horses from the livery barn, Mark, the Kid and Waco had ridden out of Mulrooney along the westbound trail. They had halted sufficiently far from their destination to avoid being heard by anybody who might be occupying the buildings. Then, being the one most competent to perform the task, the black dressed Texan had continued on foot to reconnoitre.

'I *knowed* they would be,' Waco declared. 'Seeing's how Belle was slick enough to get by me without me seeing she wasn't what she looked to be – '

'What *you* know doesn't mean no more than spit in the pot to stop it boiling,' the Kid interrupted. 'You couldn't be counted on to see a whole herd of buffalo was they to make out they was prairiedogs.'

'I was hoping Tiny wouldn't be with them,' Mark put in bitterly, before the blond youngster could object to the slander.

'Well now,' the Kid answered. 'Seeing's how he's sat there on the floor 'n' tied to a pole's holding up the roof, it could just be he isn't, intentional like.'

'Which strikes me's if he's not there 'cause he wants to be,' Waco claimed, as if making a pronouncement that had failed to occur to his companions.

'I *knew* they've'd had to slicker him into helping them!' asserted the blond giant, sounding relieved. 'Can we get to them, Lon?'

' 'Most easy enough,' the Kid drawled, exuding what appeared to be a mild hopefulness, although it did not strike either of his companions in such a favourable light. ' 'Cepting for just one itty-bitty thing, that is.'

'How "itty" and how "bitty"?' Mark inquired, deducing from his Indian dark amigo's demeanour that the problem was far from trivial.

'There's just one jasper outside,' the Kid explained. 'He's dressed like an undertaker and sat on the front porch nursing a scattergun like times're bad 'n' he's figuring on making his-self some business.'

'That don't sound mountain-high dangerous,' Waco commented, despite sharing the blond giant's estimation of the situation's gravity.

'Nope,' the Kid conceded. 'And nobody's watching the back 'n' other sides, neither. So I snuck up and right careful eased the blanket they've got covering the window open a mite. The rest of 'em are all in the front room nice's you could ask for. Trouble being, there's nowhere else in the whole son-of-a-bitching house's we could get in without making so much noise they'd know somebody was coming.'

'So why don't we 'n's just drift along there and throw

down on them through the window?' Waco suggested, ignoring the fact that the solution would not prove so simple or his slender *amigo* would already have done it.

'There's two of them sat with handguns lined on Tiny fit to make a body figure they're either right distrustful, or scared the shit of him,' the Kid answered, confirming the youngster's supposition. Gesturing with the brass-framed Winchester Model of 1866 rifle in his right hand, he went on, 'Which they were too far apart for me to've stopped 'em both at once. Happen I'd've showed myself, no matter which I'd've throwed down on, the other would've been able to make wolf bait[1] of ole Tiny afore I could turn this ole yellow-boy of mine on him.'

'Shucks!' Waco ejaculated. 'Who wants things *too* easy?'

'*We* do!' Mark and the Kid declared simultaneously.

'That's the worst of you old timers – !' the youngster began.

'The worst of *you* is likely to get chomped, whomped and stomped happen you don't keep shut!' the blond giant warned, knowing the light-hearted comment masked a genuine concern for Tiny Crumble's welfare.

'He doesn't have no *better* for you to get the worst of,' the Kid protested, sharing his big *amigo's* point of view with regards to the youngster's motives.

'Damned if I shouldn't've thought of *that*,' Mark said drily. 'And, talking about thinking, when're *you-all* going to figure some way for us to get in there and save Tiny? I've promised Belle I'll get back as quick as I could.'

'God damn it!' the Kid groaned. 'Why *me*?'

'That's for sure, Mark,' Waco supplemented. 'He only goes to find out what's wrong, not to figure on ways of putting it right.'

'You're wrong, like always,' the Kid informed the youngster, giving off an aura of patient martyrdom. 'I know just what to do.'

'You figuring on telling us?' the blond giant demanded.

'Why sure,' answered the Kid. 'There's but one way I conclude'll give us a chance of getting the drop on them and

[1] For the benefit of new readers: to 'make wolf bait' is a colloquial term for killing, arising out of the practice of shooting an animal and poisoning its carcase as a means of ridding a range of wolves and other unwanted predatory creatures. J.T.E.

saving Tiny from getting all shot to doll-rags while we're doing it.'

'Trust you-all to be giving *me* the dirty chore,' Mark growled, after the Indian-dark Texan had described what he had discovered and had made proposals for dealing with the situation, although he realised that he alone was capable of carrying out the task to which he was assigned. 'But it just *might* work.'

'*Might's* the word for it,' Waco seconded, sharing the blond giant's confidence that the scheme was practical, in spite of the way in which the reply had been worded.

'Anyways,' Mark continued, studying the youngster with a look of disdain. 'It'll give Tiny a better chance than anything else I've heard.'

'You haven't heard *me* yet,' Waco objected.

'We've been doing nothing else for weeks now,' Mark answered. 'Which I'm still waiting to hear you say *something* that makes sense. Come on. Let's go and make fools of ourselves trying out that *loco* notion of your'n, Lon.'

'I hope Belle's asleep when you get back and don't wake up until it's time for her to pull out of town,' the Kid replied, and went to slide the rifle into its boot attached to the left side of the white stallion's saddle. 'I don't reckon's I'll be needing my ole yellowboy this time around.'

While the black dressed Texan was making the decision with regards to his armament, his companions hung their hats by the *barbiquejo* chinstraps on the low horns of their double girthed range saddles.[2] Concurring with the Kid's assessment of the needs of the situation, neither of them supplemented his brace of Army Colts with his rifle. Each knew they would have failed to achieve their primary purpose if the longer range offered by the Winchesters should be required and, by failing, they would in all probability have caused Tiny's death. With their simple preparations

[2] For the benefit of new readers: because the word 'cinch' has Mexican connotations, the majority of Texans employ the term 'girth' – generally pronounced 'girt' – for the broad, short band made from coarsely woven horsehair, canvas, or cordage and terminated at each end with a metal ring and which, together with the latigo, is used to fasten the saddle on a horse's back. As Texans tied the end of the lariat to the saddlehorn when roping, instead of using a 'dally' which could be slipped free in an emergency, their rigs had two girths for greater security. J.T.E.

made, they set out on foot. Having been trained to stand still when the reins were left dangling free, the horses were left 'ground hitched' in that fashion and had no need to be tied.

Guiding the blond giant and the youngster towards their destination by a circuitous route, the Kid had no doubts over either's ability to carry out the tasks which were allotted to them. As he knew, Mark was a skilful stalker[3] and, during their short acquaintance, Waco had also proved capable of silent movement when the need arose. Their competence was demonstrated by the fact that, with no better illumination than was offered by a quarter moon, neither made any noise while approaching the house. Arriving from the side on which the Kid had carried out his reconnaisance, they were just as successful as he had been earlier in preventing Arnold Kilburn from detecting their presence.

'He's still on the front porch, the miserable looking son-of-a-bitch,' the black dressed Texan announced in a whisper, having peered cautiously around the end of the building. 'But, way he's sitting so peaceable, he for sure don't know *we* are here. Can you-all get through, Mark?'

'Just about,' the blond giant assessed in an equally quiet voice, from where he was kneeling by the wall. 'But don't reckon you're going to get away with giving *me* this god-awful chore. *You're* going to have to pay to get my clothes cleaned.'

'You-all should get a gal like Babsy,' Waco announced, *sotto voce*. 'She does all my washing for free.'

'And I thought she was smart!' the Kid sniffed. 'Go do what I told you 'stead of boasting.'

While the latter part of the whispered conversation was taking place, Mark had turned all his attention to performing his specific and vitally important duty. Like many houses of the period, the Grenley family's former living accommodation was built with its floor raised about three foot above ground level in an attempt to keep out mice and other unwanted creatures. While the gap had originally been covered with a lattice of thin and decorative wood, several sections had broken away. Moving with great care, he began to ease himself through one of the holes. As he disappeared

[3] An occasion when Mark Counter put his ability at stalking to good use is described in: *THE HIDE AND TALLOW MEN*. J.T.E.

beneath the building, the Kid walked past so as to go around the building and keep watch on Kilburn from the other side. Drawing and cocking the right hand Colt, Waco went to the front corner ready to deal with the lookout if he should come that way for any reason.

Wriggling forward on his stomach, the blond giant found that the Kid had been correct when describing the conditions he was likely to encounter. Above him, the floorboards creaked to the weight of the occupants and, although as yet not clearly enough for him to make out what was being said, he could hear them talking. However, chinks of light seeped through the cracks and served to guide him towards the room in which they were located.

Although he could hear nothing to indicate his presence had been detected, Mark did not underestimate the dangers which he might face. There was more than criminals involved in the risk, desperate as they had proven themselves to be. Rattlesnakes frequently made their homes under buildings, as did a variety of animals and birds, particularly after the property had been abandoned by human beings for any length of time. Should any be present, even if harmless, they could make enough noise to attract the attention of the criminals.

As the blond giant continued his steady advance, there were a few faint scuffling noises from the surrounding blackness. They were not, he was relieved to hear, the harsh and menacing buzzing caused by a rattlesnake vibrating the horny discs at the tip of its tail in warning. Nor did they suggest they might have been made by a bobcat, raccoon, or skunk, any of which could prove a formidable antagonist at such close and restricted quarters.

At last, Mark attained the position he was making for. Estimating that he was about in the centre of the room, he halted. Easing himself slowly and cautiously on to his hands and knees, with his shoulders pressing lightly against the floorboards, he waited. Almost a minute went by before he heard what sounded like the cry of a whippoor-will from the direction of the opening through which he had gained access. He knew it was made by Waco in response to a similar signal announcing the Kid was in position. However, he was only to reply – hoping the Easterners above him did not know sufficient about natural history to suspect the truth – if he had failed to reach the point from which he was to play his part. Being there, he kept quiet and slowly counted to twenty to allow the youngster to reach the side window.

Reaching the end of the count, the blond giant began to thrust himself upwards with all his might!

* * * * *

'Haven't you done it yet?' Terry Rushton demanded, turning his gaze from Tiny Crumble and looking across the room.

'Does it look as if I have?' Oswald Nolly answered in tones of asperity, having removed the stethoscope from his ears and straightened up to mop the freely flowing perspiration from his face.

Although the gang had been successful in leaving Mulrooney without being challenged, just as successful as Gilbert Tamar had been while collecting Tiny Crumble's Sharps Ole Reliable rifle from the room at the back of the Fair Lady Saloon, the rest of their plans had fallen badly behind schedule.

Even without the addition of the bearded giant's far from inconsiderable weight, the horse could not have pulled the buckboard at more than a walk. However, to create a further delay, it had thrown a shoe on the outskirts of the town and had been reduced to an even slower pace. So it had been almost three o'clock in the morning before they reached their destination.

Being uncertain of how long the effects of the drugged drink would last, Nolly had insisted that they took their unconscious victim into the house and fastened him with his back to a post which was being used to support a sagging portion of the roof. With this done, confronted by the task of transferring the safe from the vehicle to the sitting-room so it could be worked on under a light thereby avoiding the chance of attracting unwanted attention, they had wished they could have called upon his great strength to assist them.

Finally, when Nolly had set about opening the safe, he had found that discovering the combination of the lock was a much more difficult task than he had anticipated. Nor had the delicate task been made any easier by his accomplices, who were all sitting around the room with the exception of Arnold Kilburn who was on watch outside, repeatedly breaking his concentration by asking how things were going.

'We should've blown the goddamned door off in the first place!' Rushton snarled, squatting on his heels with his back against the right side wall. He received mutters of concurrence from Boris Miscowitz and Gilbert Tamar.

'I would have, if any of you smart-assed bastards could have told me how to do it quietly!' Nolly answered, losing his pompous way of speaking as his anger rose. 'And, even if we'd got anything to do with it, I'd still open the goddamned thing the way I'm *trying* to now. It's likely the marshal will have found out what's happened by now and the sound of an explosion would bring him straight out here to u –'

'Hey!' Tamar yelped, bringing the furious tirade to a stop. Without quitting his heel-squatting posture to the left of the front door, he started to raise his Colt Cloverleaf revolver in a threatening fashion as he continued, 'What're you doing?'

'I'm getting just a mite cramped sitting like this,' Tiny Crumble replied, the question having been directed at him as he made a movement. 'Can I stand up?'

'Like hell you can!' Rushton snapped, gesturing with the weapon of the same type he was holding.

'Let him, if he can, Ossie,' Charlotte Solikin requested, from where she was lying on a couple of blankets near the safe. 'It can't do any harm.'

'Go ahead,' Nolly authorised, mainly because of Rushton's refusal. 'But don't think we're going to loosen the rope if you can't.'

'And don't try nothing when you're up!' Tamar warned, as Tiny began to rise. 'Because, if you look like you're even *thinking* of trying to, you'll be dead.'

'I don't know why the hell he isn't already!' Rushton complained, scowling resentfully at the rebuttal.

None of the gang paid any attention to what seemed to be the plaintive call of a whip-poor-will from close to the right hand side of the building. Nor did they show the slightest interest when a similar sound came from outside on the left.

'I told you why the last time you wanted to!' Nolly responded savagely, finding the younger man's attitude growing increasingly irksome. 'Those Texans have a reputation for standing by their friends and he comes into that category. So, if he shows up dead, I want them to know the Pink-Eyes have done it. That way, they won't come looking for us. From all I've heard of them, I'd rather have all the Pink-Eyes and U.S. marshals in this whole country after my blood.'

'To hell with them!' Rushton snorted, ignoring the fact that Tiny was now standing up. 'How the son-of-a-bitch are they going to find us?'

The question was, if not answered, at least rendered pointless at that moment!

There was a splintering crackle of breaking timber and Mark Counter literally burst into view through the floorboards!

Even as he was rising, the blond giant's hands dipped to the ivory butts of his Army Colts. Yet, in spite of the speed with which he was moving and the consternation his dramatic appearance was causing most of the room's occupants, he realised that his life and that of his new found friend was still dependent upon his two *amigos* being able to carry out their parts of the scheme.

Rushton and Tamar were not so sufficiently surprised that they were frozen into immobility, but were starting to raise their revolvers and get up. Despite being equally startled, Nolly was sending his right hand flashing beneath the left side of his jacket to where a Colt Pocket Pistol of Navy Calibre – a revolver for all its name – reposed in a shoulder holster. Snarling in alarm and fury, Miscowitz thrust himself erect from where he had been sitting not too far from Rushton and snatched at the Army Colt tucked into his waistband. For her part, while coming to a sitting position, Charlotte did nothing more than scream.

However, the men were too widely scattered around the room for Mark to be able to deal with all of them before some were opening fire at him!

CHAPTER FIFTEEN

YOU LOOK LIKE YOU'RE WORRIED

Hearing the commotion inside the house, as Mark Counter was erupting through the floorboards, Arnold Kilburn lunged out of the dilapidated swing-seat upon which he was sitting and spun towards the front door. While he was doing this, almost as if blossoming out of the ground at the entrance to the porch, a black clad figure rose and sprang in his direction.

Although the lookout had not been performing the duty in a thorough – or even adequate – manner to the Ysabel Kid's way of thinking, the Kid had decided against trying to approach along the porch. Instead, after having given the call of a whip-poor-will to inform Waco that he had reached the other end of the building, he had wriggled silently across the ground in front of it. Having seen what he was doing and retiring to the window, the youngster had responded to the signal. From the next sounds to come to his ears, the Kid deduced that the blond giant was justifying his confidence and creating a most useful diversion.

The instant that the black dressed Texan's forward foot alighted on the porch, he discovered just how accurate his conclusions about the impossibility of walking along it silently had been. Creaking under his weight, the boards upon which he alighted alerted his intended victim to the danger.

Throwing a glance over his shoulder, Kilburn gave vent to a startled and profane exclamation. However, he did not restrict himself to merely speaking. Instead of carrying out his intention of entering the building to investigate the disturbance, he started to reverse his direction with the intention of turning the shotgun upon the menacing figure which was confronting him. For all his lugubrious appearance, he acted with remarkable speed.

With the matched Colts flowing from their contoured

holsters at lightning speed, their hammers clicking back to fully cocked under the impulsion of trained thumbs as the eight inch barrels were clear aand tilting upwards, Mark glimpsed the blanket over the window being jerked aside by Waco. Under the desperate circumstances, he had no time to spare for watching what further action the youngster might be contemplating. Instead, aiming at waist level and by the kind of instinctive alignment only a master gun fighter could employ with any hope of success, the forefingers – which had entered the triggerguards in as safe a fashion as his thumbs cocked the hammers – tightened to fire the revolvers almost simultaneously at the fastest moving of his would-be assailants. Caught in the left side of the chest by the two .44 calibre bullets, Terry Rushton was slammed against the wall and the Colt Cloverleaf flew undischarged from his grasp.

An instant after the blond giant's Colts cleared leather, Waco thrust his right hand through the window. What he saw warned him that Mark was in deadly danger. Sighting swiftly along the seven and a half inch barrel of his weapon,[1] he squeezed off a shot which drove its soft round lead ball into the centre of Gilbert Tamar's forehead. Even while his thumb was cocking the hammer on the recoil, he realised he had made the wrong choice.

Or rather, no matter what selection the youngster had made, it was insufficient to cope with the way the situation was developing.

For all his apparently ungainly bulk, Boris Miscowitz was rising very fast and had almost liberated his revolver. What was more, Nolly's lighter calibre – yet only slightly less deadly – weapon was emerging from beneath his jacket. Possibly because they did not know what was portended by it, neither of them was showing any sign of being put off by the bloodthirsty yell which was uttered outside the front door.

Being aware of who had raised the commotion, Waco realised that the Kid was being delayed in putting in an appearance and this could prove fatal for the blond giant.

Such was the rapidity of Kilburn's response that, if it had not been for two factors, he might have succeeded in his

[1] Although the Colt 1860 Army Model revolvers intended primarily for sale to the military had barrels of eight inches in length, those manufactured for the civilian market were half an inch shorter. J.T.E.

intentions. As it was, he paid the price for being ignorant on both accounts.

Firstly, although the criminal was holding a loaded ten gauge shotgun in his hands, he lacked the basic training in its use that any moderately competent outlaw raised west of the Mississippi River should have possessed. In spite of having been given the task of lookout, he failed to take the precaution of cocking either hammer of the weapon when taking up his post.

Secondly, in spite of the way in which the Kid was dressed, Kilburn was not in contention against a white man!

As always was the case when serious danger threatened, the black dressed young Texan met it after the fashion of the *Pehnane* Comanche Dog Soldier he had been educated to be.

No more competent fighting men than the members of that élite war lodge ever drew breath and the Kid was regarded as being among the best of them by all who knew him.

Before the .729 calibre muzzles of the shotgun could be turned in the Texan's direction, or its wielder was able to consider rectifying the omission where its hammers were concerned, he let out the ear-splitting and blood curdling war whoop of a *Pehnane* Dog Soldier. Such was the implied ferocity of the sound that, despite being ignorant of its true meaning, it achieved its purpose by frightening all thought from Kilburn's head. Then, catching the twin barrels in both hands, the Kid twisted at and wrenched the weapon from the bewildered criminal's unresisting grasp before he had an opportunity to recover his wits.

'*A'he!*' the black dressed Texan grunted, like an echo to the yell.

As he was instinctively giving the traditional Comanche coup cry meaning, 'I claim it!', the Kid propelled the butt of the captured shotgun against the side of Kilburn's jaw. There was a sharp snap of bone breaking and the criminal was knocked in a staggering spin along the porch to sprawl face down and helpless. Still reacting without any conscious guidance of his motions, as he had when claiming his coup, the Kid sprang after his victim. Up swung the heavy weapon for another blow. However, before the blow was commenced he heard the shots from inside the building and realised what was happening. Turning and running towards the door, he hoped that the time he had wasted upon the clearly *hors-de-combat* criminal would not cost any of his friends their lives.

Kilburn would never know just how fortunate he had been!

It was not often that a man who attempted to kill the Ysabel Kid escaped with no more serious injuries than a broken jaw and being rendered unconscious. In fact, particularly when acting as was dictated by his training as a Comanche warrior, the results were generally fatal.

Taking in the sight of Mark's imperilled condition and realising that Waco was unable to supply the whole answer, Tiny took a very effective hand in the proceedings!

Although the bearded giant had regained consciousness before the buckboard arrived at the gang's temporary hide-out, none of them had been aware of the change in his condition. Fortunately, he had continued to lie motionless during the short while in which he was not able to think adequately. When he could, discovering he was securely bound hand and foot, he had rapidly appreciated the precarious nature of his position. Realising that only by bursting free from his bonds quickly and unexpectedly would any bid to escape succeed, he was also aware this would not be possible in his present weakened state. Yielding to the inevitable, despite being filled with rage and mortification over the way he had been tricked, he had continued to remain still. In addition to waiting for his strength to return, he had been alert for any opportunity that might arise. None had been presented, not even while he was being carried from the vehicle and fastened to the post. There had been only one slight consolation, his legs had been cut free by the girl.

Charlotte had already earned Tiny's gratitude during the journey. When her 'brother' wanted to kill him and dispose of the body, she had supported her 'uncle's' refusal to let this be done. Furthermore, when he let it become known that he was conscious, she had brought him a drink of water. Then she had given him some disturbing news and offered advice.

Following the instructions she had received from Nolly while their captive was unconscious, the girl had stated he would not be harmed providing he caused no trouble. She had claimed they would leave him alive and bound on their departure, but warned him that he would have to flee for his life when he escaped. Believing him to be a member of the gang, the peace officers would be hunting for him. Knowing how strong he was, particularly as evidence had been left to make it appear he had killed the Pinkerton operative brutally murdered by Miscowitz, they would shoot him on sight.

Still waiting for his chance to get free and, if possible, prove his innocence by capturing the real criminals, Tiny alone of the room's occupants had seen the blanket covering the window stir in a way he could not believe was attributable to the wind. There had been no sight, nor sound, to confirm his suspicions, but he was convinced that the movement was caused by some human agency. Having heard about the Ysabel Kid's prowess as a scout, he had deduced correctly the identity of the person outside. When nothing further happened, he had concluded that whoever it was had gone for help.

Just as the bearded giant was starting to wonder whether he had only imagined there were rescuers in the vicinity, his keen ears had caught the faint noises which were emanating from beneath the floorboards and he could tell they were not all being made by animals. Then he had heard what he knew to be human beings impersonating the calls of whip-poor-wills. He had not envisaged exactly what was going to happen, but felt sure something would. Wanting to drown the sounds beneath the room and distract his captors, he had obtained permission to get up. With a rope fastened from one bicep to the other across the post, he had had little difficulty in coming to his feet. Nor was he prevented from looking around and locating where everybody else was situated.

Suddenly, Tiny gave a surging heave. He had already noticed that the post was only wedged between the roof and the floor and had decided to make use of his knowledge as a means of escaping from his bonds after the gang had left, or if necessary to help him make a fight for his life should it become obvious they intended to kill him before departing.

For a moment, the post held firm!

Then it came free!

Twisting around and bending at the waist with the post

still resting along his back, the bearded giant plunged across the room like a charging bull.

Dividing his attention between Mark and Waco, Miscowitz saw the new danger just too late. Before his far from quick wits could assimilate what the sight implied, much less try to counter the threat being posed, the top of the post was driven into him under the impulsion of all the weight and recovered strength Tiny's mighty frame was capable of producing. Thrust backwards by the irresistible force, he was hurtled against the wall. All the breath was expelled from his lungs and his chest was caved in like an eggshell. Although his forefinger tightened involuntarily on the trigger of the Army Colt, its bullet flew harmlessly into the ceiling.

Having completed his draw, in spite of realising that he would be taken to trial as an accessory to the murder of the Pinkerton operative, Nolly did not offer to use the weapon he was holding. He was no coward, but neither was he a fool. Although he would be facing the death penalty for the crime, he preferred to take the chance rather than accept the consequences of trying to fight his way to freedom.

Reaching for the Colt had been an instinctive reaction, but Nolly's assessment of the way in which the situation had developed warned him it would be futile and almost certainly fatal to open fire. If he did and hit one of the Texans, the other would show him no mercy and he had already seen just how well each could shoot. What was more, he felt sure that they had at least one companion in the immediate vicinity who would avenge them in the unlikely event that he killed both. He also was convinced that there was nobody left who might come to his aid.

'Don't shoot, gentlemen!' the Bostonian requested in a surprisingly calm voice, throwing aside his weapon and raising his empty hands above his head. 'I surrender.'

Even as Nolly was making the request and announcement, he received confirmation that the savage yell he had heard outside meant the Texans were not alone. He also discovered, as he had suspected, that there was no help likely to be forthcoming from Kilburn.

The door burst open and, holding the erstwhile lookout's shotgun ready for use, the Kid sprang across the threshold.

'Just like I figured,' the blond youngster at the window

commented. 'That blasted Indian sat around on the porch until all the work was done!'

* * * * *

'You look like you're worried, *amigo*,' Mark Counter said to Tiny Crumble, as they stood on the porch and watched Waco riding in the direction of Mulrooney. 'There's no reason for you to be. Even if the girl and Nolly hadn't promised to tell the marshal how they tricked you into helping them, the way you were hawg-tied when we found you is proof that you weren't along with them of your own free will.'

Almost half an hour had elapsed since the rescue had been effected. Having been liberated, the bearded giant had replaced the post as a support for the sagging ceiling. Watched over by the Texans, Charlotte Solikin and Oswald Nolly had done what they could for the injuries sustained by Boris Miscowitz and Arnold Kilburn. The other two members of the gang, however, had been beyond any human aid. On discovering that the horse which had drawn the buckboard was lame, Mark had sent the youngster to collect their mounts. With this done, Waco was going to inform Marshal Kail Beauregard of what had happened and make arrangements for the prisoners, corpses and safe to be collected.

'It's not me I'm thinking about,' Tiny replied. 'What's going to happen to Miss Charlotte?'

'She'll go to jail,' Mark answered, thinking that the question was typical of the gentle giant. In spite of what she had helped do to him, he still did not bear the girl a grudge. 'But I don't reckon the judge will make it for too long.'

'Can you and Cap'n Dusty see he doesn't?' Tiny requested. 'She treated me pretty good out at the cabin and stood by Mr Nolly when he told the others he was going to leave me alive.'

'We'll do all we can,' Mark promised. 'But how about you-all, what are you planning to do?'

'Was figuring on buying that lil ole burro out of the money I got for my furs,' Tiny said sadly. 'Only I don't reckon I'll have enough left after I've paid for what I did to the window at the Wells Fargo office.'

'I shouldn't let *that* worry you,' Mark declared with a

smile. 'The agent'll be so pleased to get the safe back intact he won't expect you to. Fact being, we'll tell him that he should be right grateful you've shown him how easily it was for somebody to bust in. You'll get the burro all right and it'll let you tote in even more furs the next time you come.'

'Aw shucks!' the gentle giant replied, also grinning. 'I wasn't figuring on buying him to tote things. I just want him for the company.'

THE END

APPENDIX ONE

Following his enrolment in the Confederate States' Army,[1] by the time he reached the age of seventeen, Dustine Edward Marsden 'Dusty' Fog had won promotion in the field to the rank of captain and was put in command of Company 'C', Texas Light Cavalry.[2] Leading them during the Arkansas campaign, he had earned the reputation for being an exceptionally capable military raider and a worthy contemporary for the South's other leading exponents, Turner Ashby and John Singleton 'the Grey Ghost' Mosby.[3] In addition to preventing a pair of pro-Union fanatics from starting an Indian uprising which would have decimated much of Texas,[4] he had supported Belle 'the Rebel Spy' Boyd on two of her most dangerous assignments.[5]

At the conclusion of the War Between The States, Dusty became *segundo* of the great OD Connected ranch in Rio Hondo County, Texas. Its owner and his maternal uncle, General Jackson Baines 'Ole Devil' Hardin, C.S.A., retd., had

[1] Details of some of Dusty Fog's activities prior to his enrolment are given in: *Part Five, The Civil War series, 'A Time For Improvisation, Mr Blaze', J.T.'s HUNDREDTH.*

[2] Told in: *YOU'RE IN COMMAND NOW, MR FOG.*

[3] Told in: *THE BIG GUN, UNDER THE STARS AND BARS, THE FASTEST GUN IN TEXAS* and *KILL DUSTY FOG!*

[4] Told in: *THE DEVIL GUN.*

[5] Told in: *THE COLT AND THE SABRE* and *THE REBEL SPY.* Other details of Belle, 'the Rebel Spy' Boyd's career are given in: *THE HOODED RIDERS*; *THE BAD BUNCH*; *SET A-FOOT*; *TO ARMS! TO ARMS! IN DIXIE!*; *THE SOUTH WILL RISE AGAIN*; *Part Eight, Belle 'The Rebel Spy' Boyd, 'Affair Of Honour', J.T.'s; HUNDREDTH; THE REMITTANCE KID*; *THE WHIP AND THE WAR LANCE* and *Part Five, 'The Butcher's Fiery End', J.T.'s LADIES.*

been crippled in a riding accident,[6] placing much responsibility – including handling an important mission upon which the future relations between the United States and Mexico hung in the balance[7] – upon his young shoulders. After helping to gather horses to replenish the ranch's depleted *remuda*,[8] he was sent to assist Colonel Charles Goodnight on the trail drive to Fort Sumner, New Mexico, which had done much to help the Lone Star State to recover from the impoverished conditions left by the War.[9] With that achieved, he had been equally successful in helping Goodnight convince other ranchers it would be possible to drive large herds of cattle to the railroad in Kansas.[10]

Having proven himself to be a first class cowhand, Dusty went on to become acknowledged as a very competent trail boss,[11] roundup captain,[12] and town taming lawman.[13] Competing in a revolver handling competition at the first Cochise County Fair, he won the title, 'The Fastest Gun In The West', by beating a number of well known exponents of fast drawing and accurate shooting.[14] In later years, following his marriage to Lady Winifred Amelia 'Freddie Woods' Besgrove-Woodstole, he became a noted diplomat.

Dusty never found his lack of stature an impediment to his achievements. In addition to being naturally strong, he had taught himself to be completely ambidextrous.[15] Possessing

[6] Told in the '*The Paint*' episode of: *THE FASTEST GUN IN TEXAS.* Further details of General Hardin's career are given in the *Ole Devil Hardin* and *Civil War series* and his death is reported in *DOC LEROY, M.D.*

[7] Told in: *THE YSABEL KID.*

[8] Told in: *.44 CALIBRE MAN* and *A HORSE CALLED MOGOLLON.*

[9] Told in: *GOODNIGHT'S DREAM* (U.S.A. Bantam edition retitled *THE FLOATING OUTFIT*) and *FROM HIDE AND HORN.*

[10] Told in: *SET TEXAS BACK ON HER FEET* (U.S.A., Berkley edition retitled *VIRIDIAN'S TRAIL*) and *THE HIDE AND TALLOW MEN.*

[11] Told in: *TRAIL BOSS.*

[12] Told in: *THE MAN FROM TEXAS.*

[13] Told in: *QUIET TOWN, THE MAKING OF A LAWMAN, THE TROUBLE BUSTERS, THE GENTLE GIANT, THE SMALL TEXAN* and *THE TOWN TAMERS.*

[14] Told in: *GUN WIZARD.*

[15] The ambidextrous prowess was in part hereditary. It was possessed and exploited equally successfully by Dusty's grandson, Alvin Dustine

perfectly attuned reflexes, he could draw either, or both, his Colts – whether of the 1860 Army Model[16] or their improved successors, the 1873 Model 'Peacemakers'[17] – with lightning speed and shoot with great accuracy. Ole Devil Hardin's 'valet', Tommy Okasi, was Japanese and a trained *Samurai*[18] warrior and from him Dusty, along with the General's 'granddaughter', Betty Hardin[19] learned *ju-jitsu* and *karate*.

'Cap' Fog, who also inherited the physique of a Hercules in miniature, utilizing these traits to help him become the youngest man ever to attain rank as Captain in the Texas Rangers and one of the finest combat pistol shots of his era; see the *Alvin Dustine 'Cap' Fog* series for further details.

[16] Although the military sometimes claimed derisively it was easier to kill a sailor than a soldier, the weight factor of the respective weapons had caused the United States' Navy to adopt a revolver of .36 calibre while the Army employed the heavier .44. The weapon would be carried on a seaman's belt and not – handguns having originally and primarily been developed for use by cavalry – on the person or saddle of a man who would be doing most of his travelling and fighting on the back of a horse. Therefore, .44 became known as the 'Army' calibre and .36 as the 'Navy'.

[17] Introduced in 1873 as the Colt Model P 'Single Action Army' revolver, but more popularly referred to as 'The Peacemaker', production continued until 1941 when it was taken out of the line to make way for more modern weapons required in World War II. Over *three hundred and fifty thousand* were manufactured, in practically every handgun calibre – with the exception of the .41 and .44 Magnums, which were not developed during the production period – from .22 Short Rimfire to .476 Eley. However, the majority fired either .45 or .44.40. The latter, given the title 'Frontier Model', handled the same ammunition as was used in the Winchester Model of 1873 rifle and carbine.

[17]a. The barrel lengths offered were from three inches in the 'Storekeeper' model, which did not have an extractor rod, to the sixteen inches of the so-called 'Buntline Special'. The latter was offered with an attachable metal 'skeleton' butt stock so it could be used as an extemporised carbine. The main barrel lengths were: Cavalry, seven and a half inches; Artillery, five and a half inches; Civilian, four and threequarter inches. Popular demand, said to have been caused by the upsurge of action-escapism-adventure Western series on television, brought the Peacemaker back into production in 1955 and it is still in the line.

[18] The name 'Tommy Okasi' is an Americanized corruption of the one given by the man in question, who had had to leave Japan for reasons the author is not allowed to divulge, when rescued from a derelict vessel in the China Sea.

[19] The members of the Hardin, Fog and Blaze clan with whom the author has been in contact cannot, or will not, make any statement upon the exact relationship between Betty and General Hardin. She appears in:

Neither form of unarmed combat had received the publicity both would be given in later years and were little known in the Western Hemisphere at that time. So Dusty found the knowledge very useful when he had to fight bare-handed against larger, heavier and stronger men.

Part Four, Betty Hardin, in, 'It's Our Turn To Improvise, Miss Blaze', J.T's LADIES; KILL DUSTY FOG; THE BAD BUNCH; McGRAW'S INHERITANCE; THE RIO HONDO WAR, THE HALF BREED and *GUNSMOKE THUNDER*

APPENDIX TWO

With his exceptional good looks and magnificent physical development, Mark Counter presented the kind of appearance which many people expected of Dusty Fog. It was a fact of which they took advantage when the need arose[1] and at least once was the cause of the blond giant being subjected to a murder attempt although the small Texan was intended as the victim.[2]

While serving as a lieutenant under General Bushrod Sheldon's command during the War Between The States, Mark's merits as an efficient and courageous officer had been overshadowed by his unconventional taste in uniforms. Always a dandy, coming from a wealthy family and, later, given independent means in the will of a maiden aunt,[3] had allowed him to indulge his whims. His selection of a skirtless tunic had been much copied by the other young bloods of the Confederate States' Army despite considerable opposition and disapproval on the part of hide-bound senior officers.

When peace had come, Mark followed Sheldon into Mexico to fight for Emperor Maximilian. There, he had met Dusty Fog and the Ysabel Kid, helping to accomplish the former's mission.[4] On returning to Texas, he had been invited to join the OD Connected's floating outfit.[5] Knowing

[1] One occasion is described in: *THE SOUTH WILL RISE AGAIN.*

[2] The incident is recorded in: *BEGUINAGE.*

[3] One result of the bequest is described in: *Part Two, The Floating Outfit Series (Mark Counter) in 'We Hang Horse Thieves High', J.T's HUNDREDTH.*

[4] Told in: *THE YSABEL KID.*

[5] 'Floating outfit': a group of from four to six cowhands employed by a large ranch to work the more distant sections of the property. Taking food in a chuck wagon, or 'greasy sack' on the back of a mule, they would be away from the ranch house for long periods. Because of General Hardin's

his elder brothers could help his father, Big Rance, to run the R Over C ranch in the Big Bend country – and suspecting life would be more exciting in the company of his two *amigos* – he had accepted.

An expert cowhand, Mark was known as Dusty's right bower.[6] He also gained acclaim by virtue of his enormous strength and ability in a roughhouse brawl. However, due to being so much in the small Texan's company, his full potential as a gun fighter received little attention. Men who were competent to judge such matters stated that he was second only to the Rio Hondo gun wizard in speed and accuracy.

Many women found Mark's appearance irresistible, including Miss Martha 'Calamity Jane' Canary.[7] In his younger days, only one – the lady outlaw Belle Starr[8] – held

---

prominence in the affairs of Texas, the OD Connected's floating outfit were frequently sent to assist such of his friends who found themselves in difficulties or endangered.

[6] 'Right bower': second in command; derived from the title of the second highest trump card in the game of euchre.

[7] Details of some of Miss Martha 'Calamity Jane' Canary are given in the *Calamity Jane* series. Her main meetings with Mark Counter are recorded in: *Part One, 'The Bounty On Belle Starr's Scalp', TROUBLED RANGE*; *Part One, 'Better Than Calamity', THE WILDCATS*; *THE FORTUNE HUNTERS* and *GUNS IN THE NIGHT*. She also makes a 'guest' appearance, posing as Dusty Fog's wife, in *Part Two, 'A Wife For Dusty Fog', THE SMALL TEXAN* and in *THE BAD BUNCH*.

[8] How Mark Counter's romance with Belle Starr commenced, progressed and ended is recorded in: *Part One, 'The Bounty On Belle Starr's Scalp', TROUBLED RANGE*; *RANGELAND HERCULES*. Mark's section of *J.T.'s HUNDREDTH*, q.v.; *THE GENTLE GIANT*; *THE BAD BUNCH*; *Part Four, Mark Counter in 'A Lady Known As Belle', THE HARD RIDERS and GUNS IN THE NIGHT*. She also makes 'guest appearances in: *HELL IN THE PALO DURO*; *GO BACK TO HELL*; *THE QUEST FOR BOWIE'S BLADE* and *Part Six,' Miss Martha 'Calamity Jane' Canary in 'Mrs Wild Bill', J.T.'s LADIES'* We have occasionally been asked why it is that the Belle Starr we describe is so different from the photographs which appear in various books. The researches of fictionist genealogist Philip José Farmer – author of, among numerous other works, *TARZAN ALIVE, A Definitive Biography Of Lord Greystoke* and *DOC SAVAGE, His Apocalyptic Life* – have established that the 'Belle Starr' in our works is not the same person as another equally famous bearer of the name. However, the Hardin, Fog and Blaze clan

his heart. It was not until several years after Belle's death that he courted and married Dawn Sutherland,[9] who he had first met on the trail drive led by Colonel Charles Goodnight, q.v., to Fort Sumner, New Mexico.[10]

---

have asked that we and Mr Farmer keep her true identity a secret and we intend to do so.

[9] Two of the great grandchildren resulting from the union between Dawn Sutherland and Mark Counter, Deputy Sheriff Bradford 'Brad' Counter and James Allenvale 'Bunduki' Gunn, achieved considerable fame on their own behalf. Details of the former's career as a peace officer are recorded in the *Rockabye County* series, covering various aspects of law enforcement in contemporary Texas and the latter's life story is told in the *Bunduki* series.

[10] Told in: *GOODNIGHT'S DREAM*, q.v. and *FROM HIDE AND HORN*.

APPENDIX THREE

Raven Head, only daughter of Chief Long Walker, war leader of the *Pehnane* – Wasp, Quick Stinger, or Raider – Comanches' Dog Soldier lodge and his French Creole *pairaivo*,[1] married an Irish Kentuckian adventurer, Sam Ysabel, but died giving birth to their first child. Baptised 'Loncey Dalton Ysabel', the boy was raised after the fashion of the *Nemenuh*.[2] With his father away on the family's combined businesses of mustanging – catching and breaking wild horses – and smuggling, his education had largely been left in the hands of his maternal grandfather.[3] From Long Walker, he had learned all those things a Comanche warrior must know: how to ride the wildest, freshest caught mustang, or make a trained animal subservient to his will when raiding – a polite name for the favourite pastime of the male *Nemenuh*, stealing horses – to follow the faintest tracks and just as effectively conceal signs of his own passing;[4] to locate hidden enemies, or keep out of sight himself when the need arose; to move in silence through the thickest cover and on the darkest nights; to know the ways of wild creatures[5] and, in some cases, imitate their calls so that even others of their kind might be fooled.

[1] *Pairaivo:* first, or favourite, wife. As in the case of other Comanche names, this is a phonetic spelling.

[2] *Nemenuh:* 'The People', the Comanches' name for their nation. Members of the other Indian races with whom they came into contact called them, frequently with good cause, the *Tshaoh*, the 'Enemy People'.

[3] Told in: *COMANCHE.*

[4] An example of the Ysabel Kid's ability to conceal his tracks is given in: *Part One*, '*The Half Breed*', *THE HALF BREED.*

[5] An example of how the Ysabel Kid turned his knowledge of wild animals to good use is given in: *Part Three, The Floating Outfit series* (*The Ysabel Kid*) *in* '*A Wolf's A Knowing Critter*', *J.T.'s HUNDREDTH.*

The boy had proved an excellent pupil in all the subjects. He had inherited his father's Kentuckian rifle shooting skill and, while not *real* fast on the draw – taking slightly over a second to bring out and fire his weapon, whereas a top hand could practically halve that time – he performed passably with his Colt Second Model Dragoon revolver. He had won his *Pehnane* man-name, *Cuchilo* – Spanish for 'knife' – by his exceptional skill in wielding one. It was claimed by those who were best qualified to know that he could equal the alleged designer in performing with the massive and special type of blade which bore Colonel James Bowie's name.[6]

Joining his father on smuggling expeditions along the Rio Grande, the boy had become known to the Mexicans of the border country as *Cabrito*; a name which, although meaning a young goat, had arisen out of hearing white men refer to him as 'the Ysabel Kid' and was spoken *very* respectfully in such a context. Smuggling did not attract mild-mannered pacifists, but even the roughest and toughest of the bloody border's brood had soon come to acknowledge it did not pay to rile up Sam Ysabel's son. The Kid's education and upbringing had not been calculated to develop any over-inflated sense of the sanctity of human life. When crossed, he dealt

[6] Some researchers claim that the actual designer of the knife was James Bowie's eldest brother, Rezin Pleasant. It was made by the master cutler, James Black, of Arkansas. (A few authorities state it was manufactured by Jesse Cliffe, a white blacksmith employed on the Bowie family's plantation in Rapides Parish, Louisiana)

[6]a As all James Black's bowie knives were hand made, there were variations in their dimensions. The specimen owned by the Ysabel Kid had a blade eleven and a half inches long, two and a half inches wide and a quarter inch thick at the guard. According to W.D. 'Bo' Randall of Randall Made Knives, Orlando, Florida – a master cutler and authority on the subject – Bowie's knife weighed forty-three ounces, having a blade eleven inches long, two and a quarter inches wide and three-eighths of an inch thick and his Model 12 'Smithsonian' bowie knife is modelled on it. One thing all 'bowie' knives have in common is a 'clip' point, where the last few inches of the otherwise unsharpened back of the blade joins and becomes an extension of the cutting edge in a concave arc, whereas a 'spear' point is formed by the two edges coming together in symmetrical curves.

[6]b What happened to James Bowie's knife after his death in the final assault of the siege of the Alamo Mission, San Antonio de Bexar, Texas, on March the 6th, 1836 is told in *GET URREA* and *THE QUEST FOR BOWIE'S BLADE.*

with the situation like a *Pehnane* Dog Soldier – to which war lodge of savage and most efficient warriors he had earned initiation – swiftly and in an effectively deadly manner.

During the War Between The States, the Kid and his father had commenced by riding as scouts for Colonel John Singleton 'the Grey Ghost' Mosby. Later, their specialised knowledge and talents were converted to having them collect and deliver, to the Confederate States' authorities in Texas, supplies which had been run through the blockade imposed by the United States Navy into Matamoros, or which had been purchased in other parts of Mexico. It was hard and dangerous work, but never more so than on the two occasions when they had become involved in missions with Belle 'the Rebel Spy' Boyd.[7]

Soon after the War ended, Sam Ysabel was murdered. While hunting for the killers, the Kid had met Dusty Fog and Mark Counter.[8] When the assignment upon which they were engaged came to its successful conclusion, learning that the Kid no longer wished to continue the family business, either smuggling or mustanging, Dusty had offered him employment on the OD Connected ranch. It had been in the capacity of scout rather than cowhand that he was required and his talents were frequently of the greatest use as a member of the floating outfit.

The Kid's acceptance had been of great benefit all round. The ranch obtained the services of an extremely capable and efficient man. Dusty acquired a loyal friend who was ready to stick by him through any kind of danger. For his part, the Kid was turned from a life of petty crime – with the ever present danger of having his activities develop into serious law breaking – and became a most useful member of society. Peace officers and honest citizens might have found cause to feel thankful for that. His *Nemenuh* education would have made him a terrible and murderous outlaw if he had been driven to adopt a life of crime.

Obtaining his first repeating rifle – a Winchester Model of 1866, nicknamed the 'Old Yellowboy' because of its brass frame, although at first known as the 'New, Improved Henry'

[7] Told in: *THE BLOODY BORDER* and *BACK TO THE BLOODY BORDER* (U.S.A. Berkley edition retitled *RENEGADE*).

[8] Told in: *THE YSABEL KID*.

– while in Mexico with Dusty and Mark, the Kid had soon become a master of its use. At the first Cochise County Fair in Arizona, he had won the first prize in the rifle shooting competition against stiff opposition. It was one of the legendary Winchester Model of 1873's which qualified for the title, 'One of a Thousand'.[9]

It was, in part, through the Kid's efforts that the majority of the Comanche bands had agreed to come in to the reservation, following the circumvented attempts to ruin the treaty signing ceremony at Fort Sorrel[10] Nor could Dusty have cleaned out the outlaw town called 'Hell' without him.[11] He had also accompanied Miss Martha 'Calamity Canary when she went to claim a ranch she had inherited.[12]

[9] When manufacturing the extremely popular Winchester Model of 1873, the makers selected those having barrels found to shoot with exceptional accuracy to be fitted with set triggers and given a special fine finish. Originally, these were inscribed '1 of 1,000', but this was later changed to script, 'One Of A Thousand'. The title, however, was a considerable understatement as only one hundred and thirty-six out of a total production of 720,610 rifles qualified for the distinction. Those of a grade lower quality were given the name, 'One Of A Hundred', but only seven were so designated. The practice commenced in 1875 and was discontinued in 1878, allegedly because the management decided it was not good policy to suggest the Company produced different grades of gun.

[10] Told in: *SIDEWINDER.*

[11] Told in: *HELL IN THE PALO DURO* and *GO BACK TO HELL.*

[12] Told in: *WHITE STALLION, RED MARE.*

APPENDIX FOUR

Left an orphan almost from birth by a Waco Indian raid, from whence came the only name he knew, Waco had been raised as part of a North Texas rancher's large family.[1] Guns had always been a part of his life and his sixteenth birthday had seen him riding with Clay Allison's tough 'wild onion' ranch crew. Like their employer, the CA hands were notorious for their wild ways and occasionally dangerous behaviour. Living in the company of such men, all older than himself, he had become quick to take offence and well able, eager even, to prove he could draw his guns with lightning speed and shoot very accurately. It had seemed only a matter of time before one shoot out too many would see him branded as a killer and fleeing from the law with a price on his head.

Fortunately for Waco, that day did not come.

From the moment Dusty Fog saved the youngster's life, at considerable risk to his own, a change for the better had come.[2] Leaving Allison, with the Washita curly wolf's blessing, Waco had become a member of the OD Connected's floating outfit. The others of this élite group had treated him like a favourite younger brother and taught him many useful lessons. Mark Counter gave him instruction in bare-handed combat. The Ysabel Kid had shown him how to read tracks and other tricks of the scouting trade. From a gambler friend, Frank Derringer, had come information about the ways of honest and crooked members of his profession. From Dusty Fog, however, had come the most important lesson of all; when – he already knew *how* – to shoot. Dusty also

[1] How Waco repaid his obligation to his adopted father is told in: *WACO'S DEBT*.

[2] Told in: *TRIGGER FAST*.

supplied advice which, helped by an inborn flair for deductive reasoning, turned him into a peace officer of exceptional merit.[3] Benefiting from such education,[4] he became noted in law enforcement circles; serving with distinction in the Arizona Rangers,[5] as sheriff of Two Forks County, Utah,[6] and finally as a U.S. Marshal.[7]

[3] Told in: *THE MAKING OF A LAWMAN*, *THE TROUBLE BUSTERS* and *THE GENTLE GIANT*.

[4] Two early examples of how Waco profited from his education are given in: *Part Five, Waco in 'The Hired Butcher'*, *THE HARD RIDERS* and *Part Four, 'A Tolerable Straight Shooting Gun'*, *THE FLOATING OUTFIT*.

[5] Told in: *SAGEBRUSH SLEUTH*; *ARIZONA RANGER*; *Part Six, Waco series, 'Keep Good Temper Alive'*, *J.T.'s HUNDREDTH* and *WACO RIDES IN*.

[6] Told in: *THE DRIFTER* and, by inference, *DOC LEROY, M.D.*

[7] Told in: *HOUND DOG MAN*.

DOC LEROY, M.D. by J. T. EDSON

Marvin Eldridge Leroy had been on the point of leaving home to attend medical college when bushwhack lead cut down his parents. Although he was forced to abandon his plans and take a job as a cowhand, he never forgot his ambition of following in his father's footsteps and becoming a qualified doctor. Working on ranches, or driving cattle over the northbound trails to the Kansas railheads, he took every opportunity to continue his medical studies – and gradually he earned a reputation as a doctor . . . people even called him 'Doc'. There were men, women and children alive who would have been dead without his assistance. There were also men who had died at his hands – experience had made him lightning fast with a Colt . . .

0 552 10406 X – 50p

OLE DEVIL AT SAN JACINTO by J. T. EDSON

In 1835, the oppressions of Presidente Antonio Lopez de Santa Anna had driven the colonists in Texas to rebellion. Major General Sam Houston, realizing that his small force could only hope to face the vast Mexican army when conditions were favourable, had ordered a tactical withdrawal to the east.

At last, on Thursday, April 21st, 1836, Houston decided that the time had come to make a stand. The Mexican Army, fifteen hundred strong, was on the banks of the San Jacinto river: Houston, with half that number, launched the attack that would decide the future of Texas.

0 552 10505 8 – 60p

BEGUINAGE by J. T. EDSON

To protect the life of a visiting European Crown Prince from threatened assassination, the Governor of Texas could have called up the Texas Rangers, or even the United States Army. Instead, Stanton Howard obtained the services of Ole Devil Hardin's floating outfit. Dusty Fog, Mark Counter, the Ysabel Kid and Waco had handled many dangerous people in their time but they'd never met the like of the one employed by this band of conspirators to kill the Crown Prince. Acknowledged as Europe's premier assassin, Beguinage came and went unnoticed by all except the victims. And he never failed in an assignment. The only way Dusty saw of saving the Prince was to use himself as bait for a trap – knowing that when it was sprung, either Beguinage or he would be dead . . .

0 552 10769 7 – 65p

THE WHIP AND THE WARLANCE by J. T. EDSON

Having thwarted one scheme to invade Canada from the USA, Belle Boyd, the Rebel Spy, and the Remittance Kid were hunting the leaders of the plot, who had escaped and were plotting another attempt. To help them, they called upon a young lady called Miss Martha Jane Canary – better known as Calamity Jane . . . Belle, Calamity and the Kid made a good team, but they knew they would need all their fighting skills when the showdown came. For they faced leLoup Garou and the Jan-Dark, the legendary warrior maid with the warlance who, it had long been promised, would come to rally all the Indian nations and drive the white man from Canada.

0 552 10964 9 – 65p